At His Feet

JENIFER JENNINGS

Editor: Jill Monday

Scripture quotations and paraphrases are taken from the Holy Bible, King James Version, Copyright © 1977, 1984, 2001 by Thomas Nelson, Inc.

This book is a work of historical fiction based closely on real people and events recorded in the Holy Bible. Details that cannot be historically verified are purely products of the author's imagination. Any resemblance to actual persons, living or dead, or actual events is purely coincidental.

ISBN: 978-1-954105-10-2

Alan, Michael, and Deborah.
Thank you for believing in me and my writing journey.

A Note About Names

As similar names in the Bible can get very confusing, I have offered this simple reference.

Many characters share the same name, so I have often tagged their hometown or some attribute to them in order to avoid muddling the individual characters.

Some names are Biblically documented. As is the case of Jesus' brothers, whose names can be found listed in Mark 6:3 and Matthew 13:55. Yet, there is no record of exactly how many sisters Jesus had, except for the fact he had more than one (Matthew 13:56). There is also no account of Jesus' siblings' birth order. So, I have fictionalized names for three sisters and included them in the birth order to round out the family.

The disciples also add to this confusion because some of them not only share the same name within their group, but also some of them share the same name as Jesus' brothers. I have listed the disciples' names here as well. First, by what they are called in this novel, and then the addition of their other names listed in the gospels.

I've also included a few side characters who share similar names to the main characters in the hope of clearing any confusion.

~ Jenifer Jennings

Jesus' Family:

- Mary of Nazareth- mother to Jesus, wife of Joseph
- Joseph of Nazareth- husband to Mary, biological father to all his children except Jesus
- Jesus- 1st born of Mary, Son of God
- James- 2nd born, brother
- Joseph- 3rd born, brother, and namesake of his father
- Assia- 4th born, sister
- Judas- 5th born, brother
- Lydia- 6th born, sister
- Simon- 7th born, brother
- Salome-8th born, sister

Jesus' Disciples:

- Peter (Simon)- brother of Andrew, son of Jonas, fisherman
- Andrew- brother of Peter, son of Jonas, fisherman
- James- brother of John, son of Zebedee and Salome, fisherman
- John- brother of James, son of Zebedee and Salome, fisherman
- Philip- from Bethsaida
- Bartholomew (Nathanael)- from Cana
- Thomas (Didymus)- from Galilee
- Judas Iscariot- son of Simon Iscariot, from Bethany, treasurer
- Thaddeus (Judas)- son of James, from Galilee
- James- son of Alpheus (James bar-Alpheus, for

clarification.)
- Matthew (Levi)- from Capernaum, tax collector
- Simon- from Cana, zealot

Mary's Family:
- Mary of Bethany-older sister of Martha and Lazarus
- Martha-sister to Mary of Bethany
- Lazarus-brother to Mary of Bethany
- Johnathan-Mary's father
- Eila-Mary's mother

Others:
- John-only son of Zachariah and Elizabeth, (2nd) cousin of Jesus, comes to be called John the Baptist
- Aunt Mary- wife to Cleopas, mother of James and Joseph
- Cleopas- brother of Joseph of Nazareth
- Mary Magdalene- follower from Magdala
- Joanna- from Galilee
- Susanna- from Galilee

At The Feast

"In the tenth day of this month they shall take to them every man a lamb, according to the house of their fathers, a lamb for an house:"
-EXODUS 12:3

A.D. 6, Jerusalem
The Feast of Passover

The metallic smell of blood tingled Mary's nose and tongue as she neared the Temple. It mixed with the stink of entrails and turned her stomach.

The lamb in her arms must have smelled it too. It began bleating and pulling against her.

"Shh," she chided the animal.

The pressing crowd was so loud Mary could barely hear its pleas. Merchants were shouting to potential buyers. Families were desperately trying to keep track of little ones. Harlots were calling out to men traveling alone.

Mary stayed as close to her father as she could while clutching the wiggling animal against her chest.

"Keep up, children!" Johnathan yelled.

The flow of people pushed Mary around like a small boat caught in a raging storm on the Sea of Galilee. She wondered how people lived in Jerusalem year-round. Streets which were always packed were made impassable during festivals. Jews from all around traveled to Jerusalem to fulfill their religious requirements.

Mary looked over her shoulder to see Martha holding Lazarus' hand and pulling him behind her.

"We're trying, Father," Martha called. "Come now, Lazarus."

"Are we going to be late?" Mary asked.

Johnathan shook his head. "No. We'll make it." He stopped and turned around. "Come here, Lazarus."

Mary held her breath as she watched him run. Lazarus' olive skin should have been toasted by the sun, but he was pale. He was forced to stay inside most of the time by one sickness or another. Festival times were an excellent excuse to allow him to experience limited freedom. It would be her week ruined if he injured himself again.

Lazarus made it to Johnathan's arms, just as he began a coughing fit.

Johnathan patted his son's back a few times. "There now, boy." He picked Lazarus up and placed him on his broad shoulders.

"I just don't understand why he's so slow," Martha said, catching up to Mary.

"All this excitement can be a little overwhelming."

Martha adjusted her headpiece. "But it's not like we don't come here every year. He should be used to this by now."

Mary nodded as the lamb struggled in her arms. She gripped its head against her chest and took a steady breath. She felt her heart pound against the animal. She was just as nervous as the little lamb and desperately tried to calm herself. At least their fates would not be the same.

The family pushed their way through the crowded streets toward the large Temple ahead.

"Wow." Lazarus' eyes widened.

"Isn't it magnificent?" Johnathan asked.

"It looks the same as last year," Mary said.

Her father shot her a glance.

"Sorry." Mary tucked her head to avoid his gaze.

"It's so big," said Lazarus.

"Yes, it is, my boy." He put his son back down on his own feet. "We must get this lamb ready for tonight."

In the sea of people, Johnathan took the giant Temple steps two at a time as he made his way into the stream filing into the courts with his children close behind.

Mary felt the drops of perspiration on her forehead. It was spring, but the multitude of bodies in the confined area overheated her. She wished to rip her headpiece off and catch a cool breeze on her face. But it was not permissible in public and was especially prohibited in the Temple.

They stopped at the end of the Court of Women.

Mary handed the noisy lamb over to her father.

"Watch your brother," Johnathan said, heading into the Court of Men.

Martha grabbed Lazarus' hand as he tried to follow their father. "You're not old enough to go in there."

Mary watched her father walk to the half-wall which led into the open courtyard. He paused at the gate and passed the young lamb to the priest.

"Mar-mar?"

"Yes, Lazarus?" Martha asked.

"What's that man doing with our lamb?"

Martha bent down to her brother. "That's the priest. He's going to inspect it to make sure it's clean enough to have for our Passover meal tonight."

Lazarus stretched up on his toes. "What's he going to do with that knife?"

"The priest is going to sacrifice the lamb."

Lazarus looked up at his sister and then back to the priest. "Why does he have to kill it? I thought we were going to keep it."

"No, Lazarus. We only kept it for a few days."

"But I love him. I named him John, after Daddy." The young boy's bottom lip trembled. "He's been sleeping with me."

"I know, Lazarus. This is how Passover works. We choose a lamb and bring it inside our home for a few days before we bring it to the Temple. We sacrifice a spotless lamb and have a meal together to remember what God did the night He rescued our ancestors from the Egyptians. We talk about this story every year. Don't you remember?"

Lazarus shook his head as tears streamed down his dusty cheeks.

Martha used the end of her headwrap to wipe his cheeks. "Remember the angel of the Lord passed over the houses marked with blood?"

Lazarus shook his head again.

"Moses ordered Pharaoh to let the Hebrew people go from being slaves," Martha explained. "Pharaoh wouldn't. So, God sent plagues on the land of Egypt."

"Was that before all the babies were killed?"

"After. When Moses was a baby, Pharaoh ordered all Hebrew male babies to be killed because he thought our people were getting too strong. But Moses' mother hid him…"

Martha's lesson faded into the noise of the crowd. Mary watched the priest lift the knife and make a clean slice on the animal's neck. She saw the blood begin to pour out into a bowl on the table. Her breath quickened. Flashes of blood and screams tore across her mind. She shut her eyes and turned her back on the sacrifice.

"Mary?" Martha asked. She put a hand on her sister's arm.

Mary jumped. "I need to get out of here." She rushed through the Court of Women, forcing herself past dozens of bodies. Mary nearly tripped down the broad steps, but caught herself on a group of women. "Forgive me," she said. Mary reached the bottom step and entered into the stream of travelers. The open air helped her restricted breathing. She pulled on the cloth around her neck and slowed her pace. Finding shelter near a building, she took a deep breath. A waft of spikenard danced on the hot, dry air. Memories threatened to take over, but she fought them back. She breathed in the spikenard until it was the only thing she could smell. Her whole body shook.

"Mary!" Martha called.

"Here am I," Mary choked out. She cleared her throat. "Here."

"Why did you rush off like that?" Martha asked, pulling Lazarus behind her.

"Please, Mar-mar,' Lazarus wailed. "I want to go back to Daddy."

"Hush." She scowled at him. "What is it, Mary?"

"I needed some fresh air." Mary glanced down at Lazarus and forced a smile. "It was crowded in the court." She replaced her wrap over her head and around her neck.

Martha eyed her sister. "Are you well now?"

Mary nodded as she tucked the last bit of hair under the linen.

"Mary? Martha?" their Father's voice called from the crowd.

"We are here, Father." Martha waved.

Lazarus pulled away from Martha. "Daddy," he said, running toward him.

Mary noticed the wrapped cloth under her father's arm. Blood was beginning to seep through the material. She knew it contained the freshly slaughtered lamb they had led to the Temple for the Passover sacrifice. Her throat tightened and she had to look away.

"I told you three to wait for me in the Court of Women. What are you doing out here?"

"It's my fault, Father," Mary said. "Forgive me."

"We need to go. Everyone is expecting us."

"Yes, Father." Mary nodded.

Martha and Lazarus followed close behind Johnathan.

Mary kept near, but left a few paces between them and herself.

As they walked through the market street,

Mary let her nose guide her to the scent that called to her like a harlot calling to her next customer. She followed the trail towards a nearby booth.

"Perfumes! Spices!" A merchant chanted.

She stopped to stare at a few small bottles of various colors and shapes.

"Ah. The young lady has fine taste. Those are…"

"Spikenard. I know," Mary said, picking one up. She lifted it to her nose and rubbed the small vial between her hands. The strong scent released into the air. "It was my mother's favorite."

"Pretty perfume for a pretty lady. Comes from far away."

Mary enjoyed the lingering fragrance before placing it back on the table.

"No, wait. I will make you a good deal."

"I do not have any coins to offer." Mary waved him off as she walked away. Tears stung her eyes. For the first time all day, Mary was glad that most of her face was covered. "I miss you, Mother," she whispered. "Everything was so much better when you were here." She rubbed her eyes and caught up to her family. She reached Martha and linked arms with her.

"I'm excited to see everyone again," Martha said.

Mary nodded.

The family rounded a corner and stepped inside a courtyard.

"Johnathan!" A woman, obviously great with

child, called when they entered.

"Mary," he said. "It's good to see you. I have the lamb for tonight." Johnathan handed her the wrapped linen.

"Good. Good." She accepted the parcel and looked around him. "Now, where are those children of yours?"

"Children," he called.

Mary guided Martha and Lazarus into the courtyard.

"There they are," the older woman said, handing the lamb to another woman who had come up behind her. "Come here, my little ones." She reached out.

Mary ran into her waiting arms. "It's good to see you."

"And you, my dear. It is always good to see you." She tilted Mary's chin up. "Those eyes of your mother. How I miss her."

"Me too." Mary stepped aside.

"Well?" The woman asked, putting her hands on her broad hips. "Are you two going to greet me?"

Martha stepped closer to hug her, but Lazarus stayed in the doorway.

After embracing her, Martha glared at Lazarus, "Forgive our brother. He's timid."

"Well, he shouldn't be. We're practically family," Mary from Nazareth said. She was a simple woman, but carried herself with grace. She was plain and poor. Though she didn't lack in one area of her life and that was people. Her round belly held her seventh child. She bent down and coaxed Lazarus with her finger. "Don't you remember me?"

Lazarus shook his head and took a step back.

"Come in, boy," Johnathan said. "This is one of our family's oldest friends."

Lazarus stepped back inside, but came no further.

"Well, that's alright. Let's not push him." The woman put her hand on Johnathan's arm. "Children, the others are playing around the corner if you'd like to join them. The meal will be ready soon."

Johnathan followed her with Lazarus trailing several paces behind. "Where is Joseph?"

"Same place he always is, talking with the other men and being in my way." She let out a loud laugh which echoed off the mudbrick walls.

Mary and Martha made their way down the dusty street to find the group of kids.

"Martha! Mary!" Assia squealed and hurled herself into Martha's arms.

"Greetings," Martha said, hugging her friend.

"I'm so happy that you have come to join us." The young girl beamed. "Come play."

Martha followed Assia toward the large group of children.

Mary leaned up against the cool wall to enjoy the shade.

"Greetings, Mary," a voice said.

She turned to meet a set of bright eyes. "Greetings, Jesus."

He came to stand next to her. "Your family will be joining us for Passover?"

She nodded and looked away.

"Are you upset with me?"

Mary turned back to stare at him. He always seemed to be able to read her mind. The last time she saw him, he was a young boy. The person who stood before her now was walking the fine line between boy and man. His muscular arms matched his father's craftsman's build. Heat rose in her cheeks and she looked down at the sand between her sandals.

"Mary?"

"I don't know what to think of you."

"You still blame me for what happened?"

She jerked her head up. "How could it not be your fault? Your hands are stained with innocent blood and you know it."

"Mary, I-"

She held up her hand. "I've heard it before. I know what your mother tells your siblings and the rest of the families, but I know the truth about you."

Jesus sighed. "Can you find a place in your soul to forgive?"

"Can you return all those sons to the arms of their mothers? Can you bring back all the boys who should be young men fighting to free us from Roman rule? Can you?"

He shook his head. "No. I can't."

"Then how can I forgive?" She narrowed her eyes at him.

"I was only-"

"An infant. I know. Your birth brought nothing but chaos to our region. Our towns have never recovered from that night. Yes, we moved on, but the pain we carry will always linger in our hearts." Tears began to fill her eyes. "I remain unbetrothed in my fifteenth year because there are too few men to go around. And it's all your fault."

"Is there anything I can do? Anything I can say?"

Mary looked up into Jesus' gentle eyes. She shook her head. "Do you know that night is one of the strongest memories I have?"

"I can imagine so."

"I was young; too young to see such horrors." She took a deep breath and let it out slowly. Closing her eyes, Mary recounted the memory that was etched deep in her soul, "The day was beginning to turn to night. I can still smell the freshly baked flatbread and vegetable stew Mother had prepared. Father and I had eaten our fill as Mother tended to my new sister, Martha." She opened her eyes and looked at Jesus. "Martha was so tiny." She looked at the group of children playing a few paces away. "Mother was rocking her and singing one of my favorite songs when the commotion began.

"Father was the first to notice and commented

to Mother, 'Sounds as though the neighbors are wrestling a loose animal out there.'

"Mother had merely nodded as she was fixed on Martha.

"I crawled onto his lap and asked, 'Daddy?'

"He stroked my head and tried to calm me. 'There, there, Mary. Nothing to fear,' he said.

"The door to our home flew open and in charged two Roman soldiers. I had seen them before on our trips into Jerusalem. They towered over me.

" 'There,' one ordered the other. He pointed to my Mother.

" 'No!' She screamed and huddled Martha to her chest.

" 'What is the meaning of this!' Father had demanded. He set me down and stood.

" 'We have orders,' the one at the door barked.

"I noticed blood dripping from the soldier's sword." Mary choked back tears.

"Go on," Jesus said.

"The second man wrestled Martha from my mother's arms.

" 'Please, don't hurt her,' Mother pleaded at the soldiers' feet.

"He kicked her and yelled, 'Release me, woman!'

"I rushed to Mother's side to check on her. Martha began to cry in the man's arms. The soldier unwrapped Martha from her cloth and held her naked little body up for the other to see.

" 'Another girl,' he said.

" 'Let's go.'

"He handed Martha to my father and walked out behind the other soldier.

"Mother rushed to recover Martha from Father's arms and soothed her tears. 'Shh. I'm here. I'm here.' She took Martha into the next room.

" 'Daddy?' I looked up into his eyes. 'Why did they come into our home?'

"He shook his head and said, 'I don't know, but I'm going to find out.'

"I didn't wait for permission or even think to ask. I followed him out the door and into the streets of Bethany.

"People were running everywhere. My Father grabbed the nearest person's arm and asked, 'What is going on?'

" 'It's Herod's order. They are here to kill all male children two years of age and younger,' the man explained and then rushed off.

" 'Killing children?' my father's words held disbelief.

" 'Daddy,' I called to him.

" 'Mary. What are you doing out here? Get back inside. It's not safe.' He turned me around and pointed to our home.

"Just then, another Roman soldier came out of a nearby house holding a naked baby in his arms.

"A woman ran out after him screaming, 'Please! No!'

"The soldier laid the baby on the ground. The woman caught his red cape and pulled as hard as she could." Mary pulled her sleeve to emphasize her point. "Two soldiers grabbed her and held her back. The first man adjusted his armor. He held his sword high in the air and brought it down right on the neck of the screaming infant."

"The woman yelled. 'My baby! Why? My baby!'

"The two soldiers released her and moved on to the next house.

"She crawled over to her baby's body and held him in her arms. She was wailing and screaming for him.

"Then a toddler rushed past me. He was naked as well and barely able to walk. He tripped in the sand and began to cry. I rushed to pick him up," Mary said, stretching out her arms, "But a soldier beat me to him. He used his sword to silence the crying boy.

"Father ordered me to return home. I-I-I was frozen." She shook her head. "My feet wouldn't move and my eyes wouldn't blink. Screams came from every direction. Blood stained the ground around my bare feet. Young boys' bodies lay everywhere. Mothers huddled over them, refusing to be comforted." She let the tears flow freely before she wiped them away with her sleeve.

"Father picked me up and carried me inside our home. He set me down and closed the door behind himself. Mother was huddled in a corner with Martha in her arms. She was singing the same song she had been singing before the interruption. Martha was asleep again. My house was quiet as the other mothers of our town wailed under the cover of night." She took a breath to steady herself. "Roman soldiers searched every house that night. Checked every young body and slaughtered any boy under two that they could find.

"I fell asleep to the sound of soldiers' feet marching in our streets and weeping mothers. The smell of blood hung heavy in the air that wafted into our home." Mary sniffled. "The sound of innocent flesh being ripped apart made those images stick in my mind. It was daybreak before the soldiers left, convinced they had carried out Herod's order."

She looked back at Jesus, who was staring at her. "And it was all your fault. They were searching for you."

At The Table

*"And if the household be too little for the lamb,
let him and his neighbour next unto his house
take it according to the number of the souls;
every man according to his eating shall make
your count for the lamb."*
-EXODUS 12:4

Passover Night

Martha and Mary helped Elizabeth and Mary of Nazareth set the table in the large upper room above the kitchen.

"Make sure to set an extra one, girls," Elizabeth said.

"Of course," Martha said. "We wouldn't forget Elijah's place."

When all the preparations were done, a basin of clean water was passed around the table along with clean towels. Each person took his turn to cleanse his hands, and the older children helped the younger ones.

Mary reclined next to Martha and Lazarus with the other children at the end of a large table.

Zachariah cleared his throat and moved his shawl from his shoulders to cover his head. The room became silent with anticipation. He prayed, "Blessed are you, O Lord our God, King of the universe, who has created the fruit of the vine. And you, O Lord our God, have given us festival days for joy, this feast of the unleavened bread, the time of our deliverance and departure from Egypt. Blessed are you, O Lord our God, who has kept us alive, sustained us, and enabled us to enjoy this season."

Elizabeth helped Mary of Nazareth pour the first wine cups and pass them down the table.

Zachariah continued, "I am the Lord, and I will bring you out from under the yoke of the Egyptians."

Everyone took a few sips from their cups.

The refreshing drink relieved Mary's dry mouth. She met eyes with Jesus, who offered a smile. She looked down into her cup and wished his glance would find other places to look.

Taking some bitter herbs, Zachariah and Joseph dipped them together into a bowl of vinegar and saltwater. Joseph passed the bundle of herbs down the table.

When Jesus handed Mary the herbs, his fingers lingered on hers. She huffed under her breath and snatched the bundle out of his hand. She thought she caught him stifling a laugh as he turned back toward the heads of the table. Mary sniffed the bitter herbs that made her nose scrunch. She pulled a leaf off and put it in her mouth. The salt made her mouth water. She passed it to Martha.

Mary saw Assia nudge her brother Judas.

"Oh, yes. Zachariah, why is this night different from all other nights? On all other nights, we…umm…" He looked at his sister.

"We eat…" Assia helped.

"Right. On all other nights, we eat leavened or unleavened bread, but this night we only eat unleavened bread. On all other nights, we eat all kinds of herbs, but this night we only eat bitter herbs. On all other nights, we eat meat roasted, stewed, or boiled, but on this night, we only eat roasted meat." Judas took a breath and looked over at his mother, Mary of Nazareth.

She beamed while adjusting Lydia in her arm. They had been practicing the speech for weeks so Judas could participate in the tradition as the youngest one present who could speak.

Zachariah took his time recounting the stories of their people from Abraham to Moses. When he was done, he began to sing while the others joined in, "Praise the Lord. Praise, O servants of the Lord, praise the name of the Lord…"

Mary sang the familiar words of the song. After several more lines, her eyes landed on Jesus. He was singing each word perfectly, as always.

"…Tremble, O earth, at the presence of the Lord, at the presence of the God of Jacob, who turned the rock into a pool, the hard rock into springs of water," Mary turned away from him with the last line.

Elizabeth poured a second cup while Zachariah prayed, "Blessed are you, O Lord our God, King of the universe, who has created the fruit of the vine."

Mary of Nazareth placed platters of unleavened bread and roasted lamb with vegetables on the table.

"Blessed are you, O Lord our God, King of the universe, who brings forth bread from the earth. Blessed are you, O Lord our God, King of the universe, who has sanctified us with your commandments, and commanded us to eat unleavened bread," Zachariah said. He broke a piece of bread and gave it to Joseph. Together they dipped the bread into a small bowl of olive oil.

Joseph took the bread, broke a piece, and handed it to Johnathan. The flatbread was passed down the line in the same manner.

When Jesus took the bread, he broke a piece and handed it to Mary. As they dipped together, Mary's fingers rubbed against Jesus'. She felt the heat rise in her cheeks. Her heart pounded. She dipped and ate the bite as fast as she could. Then she accepted the wafer and continued the tradition down the line with Martha.

"Are you well?" Martha whispered to Mary.

"It's very warm in here." She pulled at her shawl.

"I think it's more than the heat, sister."

When Judas and Assia had dipped their pieces together, Zachariah said, "You may now enjoy the meal."

Mary stared at the platters in front of her, but she had lost the desire to eat.

Elizabeth poured the third cup around while Zachariah blessed the remaining wafers and said, "I will redeem you with an outstretched arm and with great judgments."

They drank their cups as Elizabeth went around refilling them.

Everyone replied, "Blessed are you, O Lord our God, King of the universe, who has created the fruit of the vine."

"Then I will take you as my people, and I will be your God; and you shall know that I am the Lord your God, who brought you out from under the burdens of the Egyptians," Zachariah said. "Let us sing together, 'Not to us, O Lord, not to us but to your name be the glory, because of your love and faithfulness...'"

Mary repeated the familiar words along with the others. Even the young ones were singing along. She met glances with Jesus as the last words of the song crossed her lips, "Give thanks to the Lord, for he is good; his love endures forever."

Jesus nodded.

Zachariah removed the shawl from his head while Elizabeth cleared the table. The adults eased into conversation over simple trays of fruit while the children talked of simpler things.

"Are you enjoying Jerusalem?" John asked.

"I am, cousin," Jesus said. "I hope to return more often."

"Next year you will be an adult," John said. "You and your father could make more trips together."

Jesus nodded.

"How is the building coming?" John asked. "Do you enjoy working in the quarry?"

"It's hard work," Jesus said. "But it's nice to lay one's head down at the end of a day filled with hard work."

"Father says the city of Zippori will be magnificent when it is finished."

Assia smiled at Martha. "I love coming to Jerusalem. I hope Father lets us come back every year. Especially since we get to spend time with all of our friends."

"It is nice to have all of you close by," Martha said. "Bethany is so small. Mary and I don't have many friends our age."

Mary narrowed her gaze at Jesus.

At The Temple

---

*"And when they had fulfilled the days, as they
returned, the child Jesus tarried behind in
Jerusalem; and Joseph and his mother knew not
of it."*
-LUKE 2:43

Jerusalem
Four Days After Passover

When will we be heading home to Bethany,
Father?" Martha asked.

"We'll leave tomorrow. I have some more
business in the city."

"Can we go into the market today?" Mary
asked.

Johnathan nodded. "Here," he said, reaching
into his tunic. "Take a few coins and you girls
enjoy yourself. Be back before dark."

Mary took the outstretched coins and left with
Martha.

"I really enjoyed spending time with all the
children," Martha commented on their way
through the crowded market streets of Jerusalem.

Mary shrugged.

"Why don't you and Jesus get along?"

"What do you mean?" Mary asked, without meeting her sister's questioning eyes.

"You know exactly what I'm talking about. Jesus is the eldest child of his family. Yet you ignore him like he has leprosy or some other unclean condition."

"It's something you're too young to understand," Mary said, pressing her way through the crowd.

"I understand more than you think I do."

Mary kept quiet and looked around at a nearby booth. She picked up a pomegranate and held it to her nose.

"I thought you would keep your opportunities open."

Mary paused and turned to face her sister. "Pardon me?"

"I mean, there are not many young men in Bethany. I think you and Jesus would make a good match." Martha browsed a large pile of leeks. "I've overheard Father and Joseph talking."

Mary dropped the fruit back down on the pile. "About?"

"You and Jesus being betrothed."

Mary caught her sister's stare.

"He is from a poor town. Maybe Joseph will take a reasonable dowry for you."

"I would never agree to be betrothed to Jesus," Mary said and crossed her arms.

"What's wrong with him?"

Mary shook her head. "I told you, you won't understand." She began to walk away.

"You're maddening, sister." Martha joined her side. "It's not like you have a choice anyway. Whatever Father says, you will do."

"I know." She looked away.

The two sisters made their way toward the Temple. When they entered the court of women, Martha pointed to one of the side rooms. "Is that Jesus?"

Mary looked in the direction Martha pointed. She could see Jesus sitting among a group of leaders. "What is he still doing in Jerusalem? His family left a few days ago."

"Maybe they decided to stay longer?" Martha offered.

"No. We saw them off that morning, remember?"

"But I thought he was with them."

"I'm guessing so did they," Mary said.

"Look, he is waving us over." Martha pointed. "Let's go check on him."

The two young women walked to the group.

"Forgive me, teachers," Jesus said and turned to the girls as they approached.

"Jesus," Martha called. "Why are you here?"

"Mary. Martha. Greetings," Jesus said.

"Are these your sisters?" One of the teachers asked.

"No, but they are very close friends of my

family."

The man stroked his long, gray beard. "This young man has been asking the most interesting questions."

"Jesus!" Mary turned toward the sound of a woman shouting. "I found him, Joseph. He's over here."

Joseph and Mary of Nazareth came to stand next to Mary and Martha. Jesus' mother had her hands on her hips. "Son, why have you done this to us? Your father and I have been looking for you all over the place. We were so worried about you."

Jesus calmly turned toward his parents. "Why were you looking for me? Didn't you know that I must do my Father's business?"

"What are you talking about?" his mother asked.

"It's time to come with us now, son," Joseph instructed.

"Yes, Father." Jesus rose. "Thank you for the talk, teachers." He bowed to the men and then turned to the sisters. "I hope to see you at the next Passover. Martha." He bowed. "Mary." He bowed even deeper with a smile.

"We would enjoy that very much," Martha said, returning the bow.

Mary lowered her head just enough to be accepted as a bow.

Jesus straightened and then left with his family.

"Did you see the way he was looking at you,"

Martha asked, as they rushed down the steps.

"No. He always looks like that."

"Mary, when are you going to see it?"

"See what?"

Martha pulled Mary's arm to make her look her in the face. "Jesus does care for you. Could you ever care for him?"

"How could I spend my days next to the man who caused all of our people's grief?"

"When are you going to let that go?"

"I can't. I know if it had not been for Jesus being born, our lives would be better. Our people would be strong. Romans would fear us instead of conquering us. You and I would be betrothed to men who could make our lives comfortable. Mother would still be…" Mary choked back tears.

"You can't blame all that on an infant?"

"Jesus is no infant. If he were truly the son of God, as his own mother used to claim him, then why doesn't he do something about any of it?" Mary squared her shoulders. "Instead, he chooses to play with sticks and stones and watch the rest of us suffer."

At The Grave

"For in death there is no remembrance of thee: in the grave who shall give thee thanks?"
-PSALM 6:5

A.D. 7, Bethany

Moans grew from the crowd that gathered around the front of the cave. Some of the faces were familiar to Mary, but most of them blended into each other. They were professional mourners Martha had purchased for the funeral.

She stared at the lifeless body of her father. He looked like a sleeping child that had just been tucked in for the night. Mary could see his face through the sheer burial linen, though his eyes were blocked by the thicker prayer cloth.

Mary broke her stare long enough to find the eyes of her younger brother, Lazarus. He wasn't crying, but the red of his eyes gave away that he had run out of tears for the moment. She wondered if a boy only a few years from being counted as a man by society could understand. Most may. Lazarus was different. Mary didn't think he would ever understand.

Martha stood with her arm around him as if to shield him from the pain. She had enough tears to weep for all of them.

Mary couldn't stop the thought that ran across her mind about how much Martha was holding herself back from tidying something. It never mattered what, though Martha would argue that point until the sun hid behind the horizon. When Martha's nerves got to her or she was bothered by something, she would set her hands to cleaning anything and everything that would sit still.

Both of her siblings' focus where on the body and that's where Mary allowed hers to return.

Mary's tears came and went. They came when she thought of some wonderful memory. There were many of those. They went when she grew numb to the flood of grief that threatened to take her down with it. It was not so much that the feelings left, more like she forced them down and away. Mary didn't have the patience for sadness. She was the oldest sibling, she was all her sister and brother had left, and she was entirely responsible for taking care of them now.

Glancing back over to her siblings, Mary thought of Lazarus. He would never take a wife. No family would sell a valuable commodity to someone who could never take care of her. Even though there were not many choice men left in Bethany, Lazarus would never have a chance.

Mary's eyes moved to Martha. A young

woman whose thoughts should be turning to her own betrothal and future life as a man's wife. If their father had lived longer, then Martha might have had a chance. With him gone, Mary was not going to be able to negotiate an arrangement for Martha. There were just too few men and too much competition for them to choose from.

The chants and wails grew quiet as the crowd began to thin. Mary couldn't blame them since most had been making preparations well before sunrise. The relatives would stay until the siblings went home. If Martha had anything to say about it, that would be well before sunset in order to make sure meal preparations were made for the guests before she rechecked the sleeping arrangements for the tenth time.

Mary couldn't be mad at her sister, at least Martha's work gave her some sort of peace in all types of situations. Peace had always been something that eluded Mary. Its foundation began to shift when her mother passed away. Now, the remnant was shaken to sand with both of her parents gone.

The wind changed direction and Mary caught sweet hints of the burial spices that had been rubbed into the linens. Spikenard, mixed with the other overwhelming scents, was hard to miss. Mary's mind flooded with images of her mother. Her olive skin, her almond-shaped eyes, and her wide smile.

Mom.

Mary was grateful for the overpowering scents, even if they brought with them the memories of her mother. At least, they covered the stench that would otherwise be causing the women to cover their faces with their headpieces.

Mary and Martha had spared no expense. In standard burial procedures, what they had access to would have been more than sufficient. Mary had decided that nothing could ever be enough for her father. He would not go to his grave with anything less than royal treatment on her watch.

"We only get to bury him once," Lazarus' words echoed in her mind. Martha couldn't say no to him and had agreed to the expense.

Mary watched as two large men stepped up to her father's lifeless body. It was time. They picked up the body and headed into the tomb. She paused briefly at the mouth of the cave to grab a torch off the wall so she could see in the darkness.

The mountain was huge. Her ancestors had dug deep enough into it to provide plenty of room for their legacy. Mary wondered which shelf would contain her body, but pushed the idea away.

She came upon the men just as they were placing her father's body on a shelf. The sisters had picked a high ledge as his resting place. It was right above their mother's body.

As the two men left the tomb, Martha and Lazarus came to stand by Mary.

Martha held a torch and led her brother close to the shelf.

Lazarus' whispers were meant to only be for the deafened ears of their father, but the cave walls echoed the words for Mary to hear them clearly. "I will miss you, Daddy. Don't worry, I'll take care of my sisters. I promise," he said through a cracked voice.

Mary opened her mouth to say something, but then closed it just as Lazarus turned toward them.

Martha nodded and wrapped her arm around his shoulder. They walked out of the cave.

As she watched her siblings leave, Mary remembered the news of their father's death. It had been Lazarus who found him. He was always the one who rose before any of them. Mary had joined Martha in the kitchen to begin the morning meal preparations. Lazarus had come into the room. His skin closely matched the color of a sheer cloth. The shock on his face drew the attention of both sisters.

"Father is not moving."

The words had sent Mary and her sister charging into the room where their father slept. There he lay, just as Lazarus had said.

Mary looked at her father's lifeless body lying on the shelf. She took a step closer and whispered, "Goodbye."

Turning away, she headed toward the fading light at the mouth of the cave. Before leaving the tomb completely, she pushed the lit end of her torch into the sand to kill the fire. Making sure it was out, she returned it to its place on the wall and left the cave to make her way home. She knew the men would make sure the large stone was replaced in front of the mouth so no animal would get in looking for its next meal.

"We've got to go up to Jerusalem," Martha said, months after burying their father. "It's nearly Passover."

"How can we?" Mary asked.

"Father's friends have sent word that we are welcome to join them. It will be nice to be around friends."

"Nice to sit around and watch the sadness grow large in their eyes every time they look at us?"

"Mary," Martha scolded. "They are our dearest friends. They want us to be with them."

Mary turned away.

"Think of Lazarus. It'll do him good to be around people who care about him."

Mary kept her back turned.

"Please?"

"Yes. We will go," Mary said. She turned to face her younger sister's pleading eyes. "Pack some things. We'll join the others in Jerusalem tomorrow."

Mary guided her two siblings to a familiar house in Jerusalem.

"Children." Mary of Nazareth stepped into the courtyard and fell on their necks. "It makes my heart sing to see you three." She stood and wiped her face with the cloth in her hand. "Please, join the others. They are in the upper room."

"Do you need any help in the kitchen?" Martha offered.

"Certainly, my child." She wrapped her arm around Martha. "It is always nice to have an extra set of hands."

Lazarus was already rushing up the steps.

Mary dragged her feet to the first step.

"Oh, Mary?"

Mary turned back to the older woman. "Yes?"

"Jesus is looking for you."

Mary looked back at the steps in front of her. "Just the person I don't wish to see," she mumbled under her breath.

When she reached the last step, Mary found Jesus waiting there for her.

"Greetings, Mary."

She walked past him into the room.

"I'd like to speak with you," he said, following her.

She nodded to the others in the room who

waved to her.

"Mary, did you hear me? I said, I'd like to-"

She turned to face him. "What could you possibly have to say to me?"

"Please. Don't be angry. I only wanted to say how sorry I was to hear about the death of your father."

Tears blurred her vision. "And you weren't there to mourn him."

"No," he said, bowing his head. "We had much work to do before we could travel to Jerusalem. I wish we had left sooner so that we could have been close when it happened. I know how you feel."

"You have no idea how I feel. You've never lost anyone close to you."

"Mary, God will show you the path you are supposed to walk."

"God has done nothing but take from me."

"You know that's not true."

"What else can I believe? My mother died giving birth to Lazarus. He was born small and frail and remains as such. And now," she lowered her voice. "My father is also dead. I'm the oldest. What am I going to do?"

"You are not the only one who has recently lost people they love."

Mary furrowed her brow. "I don't understand," she said, searching the room. Her eyes landed on John, Jesus' cousin, who was seated in a corner with his head leaning on the wall. She searched the room over again for his mother and father.

"John's parents are dead," Jesus answered her internal question. "After Passover, he will be sent away to live with the Essenes in the wilderness. They will take care of him."

"When did they..."

"Right before we left. They were well advanced in age before John was even born. It was just a matter of time, as it is for all of us." He looked over at her. "We were coming to Jerusalem for the feast anyway. Father promised that he would make sure the boy would be safely delivered to the Temple. The High Priest ordered that he be sent to the desert where all orphans of the Levities are sent."

"He's still young."

"Yes, but John doesn't wish to follow in his father's sandals to join the priesthood."

"What will he do out in the desert?"

For a moment, Mary saw a glint in Jesus' eyes, but it soon faded.

"John is willing to walk where God has led him.

At The House

"And the LORD, he it is that doth go before thee; he will be with thee, he will not fail thee, neither forsake thee: fear not, neither be dismayed."
-DEUTERONOMY 31:8

Bethany
Six Months Later

Mary watched the sun dance above the Mount of Olives as she remembered her parents. She had so much comfort in knowing she was able to bury them properly according to their customs and they would find honor in that simple act. Yet, she found herself with such an emptiness that she felt like a hollow shell. Somehow, she felt as if she was the one who had died and her body had not known to stop walking around.

"Mary?" Martha called.

Mary went inside to find Martha pacing around the kitchen.

"Yes?"

"Mary, I need to go to the market to buy food. Do you have any more coins?"

Mary felt the tied fold in her dress. "I have two coins. That will buy some, for now."

Martha took the money out of Mary's outstretched hand. "I will make do. We've got to figure out something. Father's money will not last long."

"I know," she nodded.

Martha adjusted her shawl over her head and grabbed a shoulder bag. "Look after Lazarus while I'm away."

"I always do."

When Martha left, Mary checked on her younger brother. "Lazarus?"

"Sister," he smiled.

She knelt on the floor beside him. "What are you doing there?"

He pointed with the stick in his hand.

She looked into the dirt to find simple drawings. "That's very good."

He continued to doodle.

She patted his head.

"Where's Daddy?"

Her eyes began to mist. "Remember? Father went to be with God."

He shook his head. "Why did he do that? He was supposed to help me finish my stool."

"I can help you," she offered.

He furrowed his brow. "You're a girl. I want Daddy to help me."

"Daddy can't help you. He's gone now."

"But I want him." Lazarus began to cry. "I

want Daddy."

"I do too," Mary said, feeling her own eyes begin to overflow with water. "But he's not coming back."

"Daddy!" he whaled.

"Shh, peace. Martha and I will take care of you."

"Where's Mar-mar?"

"She went to the market. She'll be back soon."

"I want Mar-mar!"

"Peace, Lazarus. Please," Mary pleaded.

"I want Mar-mar. I want Daddy."

She tried to hug him, but he pushed her away.

"I don't want you."

"Very well." She stood and left the room.

When Martha returned, Mary was sitting outside the front door.

"What is going on in there?" Martha asked.

"He's screaming for you and Father. Has been since you left. He wants nothing to do with me."

"Oh, Mary." Martha stormed into the courtyard. "I asked you to watch him for a short while so that I could go to the market." She set her items down on the table in the kitchen.

Mary followed. "I tried. I did try. He doesn't want me."

"Mar-mar!" Lazarus screamed and ran into Martha's arms.

"I'm home now, Lazarus. No more of that noise."

"Where's Daddy? He has to help me with my

stool."

"He has gone to be with God. Mary and I are going to take care of you."

"I don't want Mary."

"Hush that talk. Mary is your sister. You will love her as you do me." She handed him a dried fig. "We are all you have now."

Lazarus stuffed the whole thing in his mouth.

"I tried to tell him." Mary huffed.

"Mary, you have to be gentler with him." She stroked Lazarus' head. "Run along and play."

He obeyed.

Mary helped Martha put the food away.

"You know he's different."

"I know that," Mary said. "But we can't always treat him like a child."

Martha paused. "What do you think? That he'll grow into a strong man? That he will find work enough to feed our mouths?"

Mary shrugged.

"He's never going to be like other boys. Look at him," she said, motioning with her head. "He's half the size a boy his age should be. He's constantly sick. We're lucky he is still with us."

"Why has God done this to us?"

"Done what?"

"Cursed us. Our parents are gone. Our brother is-"

"Different," Martha interrupted.

"-different. We are almost out of money. No man will have us without a dowry."

Martha looked her in the eyes. "We will survive. Our family always has."

"Our family has always thrived," Mary bit back. "We come from a wealthy heritage and an even stronger lineage. Yet we are staring starvation in the face. I don't know what to do to lead this family. It feels as though God has left us. Has left me."

"God has promised to never leave us."

"Then, where is He?"

At The Market

"Luke, the beloved physician…"
-COLOSSIANS 4:14

Four Months Later

"Greetings, Mary," a husky voice called over the crowded market.

Mary turned. "Peace to you." The hair on Mary's arms stood straight on end. She could never place why, but she dreaded being around Judas Iscariot. Everything about him was dark. His skin was like cinnamon that had been left too long over a fire. His hair was like ashes. Even his eyes. They were the darkest black, she had ever seen. It was like looking into a deep cave containing creatures which only belonged in nightmares.

"An excellent selection of barley this year," he said with a grin.

Mary nodded as she fought the shiver that ran up her back.

"How is your brother?"

"Not well today." She motioned for the seller to weight out some barley. "I'm shopping for some of his favorite foods to cheer him up."

"That will be two shekels," the merchant said, holding out his hand.

Mary reached into her cloak and felt the place where she tied the coins early that morning. "Oh," she whispered to herself.

"Something wrong?" he asked.

"No. I'll only need half that."

The merchant huffed and dumped half of the barley back into the pile. "One shekel."

Mary handed him the silver coin and took the pile of grains. She placed them in her bag and began to walk to the next booth.

Judas Iscariot followed her. "And your sister?"

"She is well."

"And you? How are you?"

She paused. "I am well enough."

"You know you could be a lot more comfortable."

She turned toward him.

"I know your father didn't make any arrangements before he died concerning your betrothal."

She nodded.

"You know my family is very wealthy."

Another shiver raced up Mary's back.

"I could talk my father into making arrangements for you to come live with us."

"You mean, marry you?"

His eyebrow lifted. "Yes."

"And what of my siblings? I couldn't leave

them."

"I could possibly talk Father into Martha as well. Of course, Lazarus would have to work off all of the debt to my family. Once he is well."

"You mean as a servant?" She held her breath.

"Well, you don't think my father would be interested in marrying his oldest son off to two women and taking on the responsibility of a sick man without some kind of substantial payment, do you?"

Her stomach turned over on itself. She felt heat rise in her cheeks as the smile widened on his face. "I remember when your father was sick. When your mother had to make the choice to care for him in your home instead of sending him away to one of the colonies. My father and many of the other men in town rallied to your family's aid. We provided food. Many even forgave the debts your father had accrued once he was well again."

His face twisted for a moment before smoothing again. "That's all true, but my father is alive and well and, well, yours is…"

"How dare you." She straightened her shoulders. "My father was a good man who worked hard."

"Not hard enough to provide for you in his passing."

"I could never agree to marry someone with such a cold heart."

"You don't have much of a choice."

"Then at least I will die with honor."

"Have it your way," he said, pressing his face near hers. "One day soon they will come for your house and everything you own. You will watch your brother and sister slowly starve. And then you will die in the streets like the filthy harlot that you are." He walked away with a huff.

Mary took a deep breath and steadied her trembling hands. She would never dare to speak so boldly in public, but he had a way of crawling under her skin. She glanced around at the people who had been watching the commotion and ducked under her headpiece.

I couldn't marry a man like that. Even if it does mean certain death.

"Thank you, thank you," a woman repeated.

Mary turned to see an older woman repeatedly kiss the hands of a young man in the street.

Mary moved a little closer.

"You have saved my son."

The man pulled his hand away. "I only gave you medicine…"

Medicine. Mary moved even closer.

"…you need to make sure he takes all of it," he instructed. "Don't sell it."

"Of course," the woman said, with a deep bow.

"I'll come to check on him before I leave the city."

The woman bowed again before backing away into her home.

The young man turned and saw Mary watching him. He dipped his head and smiled.

Mary ran to him. "Pardon me, but I overheard you speaking to that woman."

"Yes?"

"Are you a physician?"

"I have been trained in medicine, yes."

"My name is Mary and my brother is sick. I know you must be extremely busy, but could you please come see my brother? He is very ill."

The man looked around. "Where is he?"

"We live in Bethany."

His shoulders slumped. "I'm afraid I can't-"

"Please. It's only a short walk from the gates."

"I can't leave-"

"Please," Mary's eyes watered. "He needs more than I can give him. I'll pay you whatever you want."

He looked around again. "As long as I can be back in the city before nightfall."

"Even if I have to borrow a cart and bring you back myself. On my honor."

"That won't be necessary." He held up his hand. "If we are going to go, then let's get going."

Mary picked up the hem of her dress and led him through the gates of Jerusalem. They reached the Mount of Olives before she realized she didn't even ask the man's name.

"Luke," he answered.

"What business brings you to Jerusalem?"

"I'm from Antioch. My family came to trade here. They enjoy the travel and finding new luxuries."

The two came upon Mary's home in Bethany within a few short hours.

"Martha," Mary called when they entered the courtyard.

Martha came in from Lazarus' room.

"Sister, this is Luke. He is a physician."

Martha bowed.

Luke returned the gesture.

"My brother is just through there," Mary pointed to the room behind Martha.

Martha stepped aside to let him pass. "Where did you find a physician?" She whispered to Mary.

"In the city. He has agreed to help."

"Mary, we don't have much money left."

Mary swallowed hard. "I know, but we only have one brother."

It wasn't long before Luke returned to the courtyard. "Can you tell me some of his history? A difficult birth?"

Mary fought the dryness in her throat. "Yes, a complicated birth. Our mother died in the process."

"I see," Luke said, rubbing the short beard on his face. "Does he get sick often?"

"Yes," Martha said. "All the time."

Luke moved to the kitchen. He dipped his hands in the cleansing vessel and then wiped them on a nearby cloth.

"Our brother has always been a bit different," Martha offered in the silence. "He has always seemed younger than he is. Always had a difficult time being able to communicate well. And sick. Always sick."

"I see," he said, without looking up from the cloth in his hands.

"Can you help our brother?" Mary asked.

Luke laid the cloth on the table and met the sisters' eyes. "I can give him something for the fever, but I'm afraid the rest is beyond my training."

"I thought you said you were a physician." Mary stepped toward him.

"I am a humble servant trained to care for the family I serve," Luke explained. "Yes, I do have medical training, a great deal of it, but I am not God that I can change the internal workings of a man."

Martha turned away and went into Lazarus' room.

"You see," Luke continued. "Your brother's issues do not lie in the realm of what I can treat. The body goes through quite a strain during birth. If it was as complicated as you say, many of his body's functions could have been damaged beyond repair. Any of which could cause complications."

"What kind of complications?"

"The head is a big area of concern. The heart, lungs, and other organs could also have been damaged," he said, working his hands down his body, stopping at each spot for emphasis. "Even before he was born, his mother's distress could have caused a host of problems for him."

"You're saying he's not going to get better."

"What I'm saying is that I can treat some of the symptoms he has now. No one but God will cure him of whatever causes them all. You say your mother died in childbirth, where is your father?"

"Gone as well."

"I see. So, it's just the three of you?"

"Yes." Mary looked toward Lazarus' room. "We take care of our brother."

Luke leaned on the table. "You'll have to make some changes around here and get him some better food."

"All of that costs money."

"I can only treat what I can. I can also show you some tricks to help keep him well, but it doesn't mean he will never get sick. The better you care for his environment and his body, the less likely he will be to fall ill."

"I would be grateful for any help."

For the next hour, Mary followed Luke around every corner of their home. She memorized everything he said.

"If you do all that, your brother might stay well. Like I said, I cannot guarantee anything."

"I appreciate your advice."

Luke nodded. "I must get back to Jerusalem."

"Of course."

"Take this." He pulled a vial from his shoulder bag. "Give him a sip with each meal until he is feeling better. I'm sorry I can't come back to check on him."

"You've done so much for us." Mary accepted the vial. "And here is your payment," she said, holding out a few coins.

He took them and put them in his coat. "I wish you and your brother the blessing of God. Know he will be in my prayers."

"And you will be in ours, Luke."

Mary showed the physician out into the street before she took the vial and some barley bread into Lazarus' room.

"What did he say?" Martha asked, keeping her eyes on their brother.

"We've got to work extra hard to keep up the housework. We've got to get him more fresh vegetables and keep him clean." She handed her the food and vial. "He needs to take a sip of this with food."

Martha broke a piece of the wafer and uncorked the vial. "Lazarus," she sang softly. "Time for some food."

Mary lifted his head slightly while Martha put the piece of bread and poured some of the liquid into his opened mouth.

"That's good, brother. Chew and swallow. This will help you feel better." Martha replaced the cork and put the vial into her dress pocket. She then took a bite of the wafer for herself.

"Let's let him rest," Mary said. "We need to talk."

Martha nodded. "We will be in the next room if you need us, brother."

Lazarus moaned.

Martha followed Mary into the next room that the two sisters shared. "I don't mind the extra work," Martha said. "You know me. It's the money that concerns me."

"I know," Mary replied.

"We are barely surviving. How are we supposed to get the best for Lazarus?"

"I've been thinking the same thing."

"How much do we have left?"

"Not much." Mary rubbed her forehead. The weight and pressure of their situation hung on her delicate body.

"What if we sold the house?"

Mary's head popped up. "I already gave up Mother's garden, I'm not giving up Father's house."

"We've sold everything else. The storage downstairs is nearly empty as well."

"There is one thing I haven't sold yet," Mary said more to herself than to her sister.

"What?"

The words of Judas Iscariot danced around in Mary's mind, "You will die in the streets like the filthy harlot that you are." *Me. I haven't sold myself.*

Mary had seen them several times on their trips into Jerusalem. Pretty girls with bright colored robes. Every inch of their faces painted. Men paid and seemed to pay well.

"Mary?" Martha's voice called her attention

back.

"I think I've got a plan, but you must look after Lazarus while I'm gone."

"Is there anything I can do to help?"

"Start cleaning. Luke said this place needs to be cleaner than the Temple."

Martha nodded and rushed to begin her work.

Mary rose slowly and went into the next room. Lazarus lay sleeping on his bedroll.

"Rest well, dear brother. I will make sure you are cared for," she said and then stepped into the open courtyard. Night was coming and she needed to try out her plan before she lost her nerve.

"Mary," Martha yelled.

Mary heard her sister moving around in the courtyard and rolled over.

"Mary," Martha called again.

She groaned.

"Get up. It is well past sunrise. I expect this thing of Lazarus, but not from you."

She pulled the blanket over her head.

"Mary!" Martha came into the room and snatched the blanket off Mary. "You get up right now. There is too much to do for you to sleep all day."

"Martha, have mercy. I'm tired," Mary said and reached for the blanket.

"I don't understand why you are so tired. It's as if…" Martha paused and then knelt down beside Mary. "Are you ill as well?" She put her palm on Mary's face.

"No, I'm not ill." She pushed Martha's hand away.

"Let me see your eyes." Martha lifted Mary's face to the sunlight. "Mary! What is all over your eyes?

"Coloring."

"Why do you have coloring on? Your eyes are all red."

"I told you, I'm tired." Mary rolled over.

Martha pulled her back. "You talk to me this moment."

"You're not my mother."

"No, I'm not your mother. I'm your sister. And I care for you."

Mary sat up. "Hand me my cloak."

Martha reached for the garment and handed it to her.

"I tried to find a way to tell you before I left last night, but at least I can show you." Mary reached for the purse she tied into her cloak. She dropped the bag into Martha's lap.

Martha picked it up and felt it. "What is this?"

"Coins, sister."

"Where did you get them from?"

"I earned them."

Martha shook her head. "Earned them how?"

"Martha, I…" She looked down at her sister's

feet. "I…"

"Oh. Mary, no."

Tears blurred her eyes. "I had to. Father's money was running out and Lazarus was so sick. It was the only thing left I could do to provide for you two."

"We could have found another way."

"No." Mary shook her head. "I wasn't going to have Lazarus die as a servant."

"Servant? What are you talking about?"

"Judas Iscariot. He offered a betrothal to me."

"That's wonderful. His family is wealthy."

"I know, but I couldn't leave you to care for Lazarus alone."

"I would have managed."

"How? You have no way to bring coins into the house."

Martha shrugged. "Maybe I would have tried to find work in the city."

"Lazarus needs constant care when he is sick. Could you take care of him and work in the city?"

Martha shook her head.

"He offered to marry both of us."

"He did?"

"Yes, as long as we handed over Lazarus as a servant to pay our dowries and his board for living with their family."

"That's absurd."

"That's what I said."

"Lazarus wouldn't be able to contribute much. If he got sick, he wouldn't be able to work. Then he'd have even more debt to work off if they paid to treat him."

"Exactly why I turned him down."

Martha rocked back on her heels. "I don't know what to say."

"I know." She hugged her. "That's why I did what I did."

"It's awful to think of you having to do that for us."

"It was very difficult, but I think I'll get better. The money is good. You would be surprised how many travelers there are in Jerusalem who are willing to pay. I think we can survive."

Martha brushed Mary's hair away from her face. "You need some rest. I'll bring you something to eat later."

"Thank you, sister," Mary said and laid back down on her small bedroll.

"No. Thank you, sister."

At The River

*"In those days came John the Baptist, preaching
in the wilderness of Judaea,"*
-MATTHEW 3:1

Sixteen Years Later

Mary brushed some loose dirt from her brightly colored dress before she reached to adjust her headpiece.

"Where are you going so early?" Martha asked when Mary entered the kitchen.

"There was word in the city last night that John is preaching near the Jordan." She gathered some fruit and bread into her pouch.

"John?"

"You remember Elizabeth and Zachariah's son."

"Oh, yes. John."

"He has left the community to teach. I want to hear him."

"Give him my best."

"I will. How is Lazarus this morning?"

Martha wiped her hand on a rag. "He seems

well. He wanted to go work in the garden."

"Do you think that wise?"

"He doesn't get to leave the house much. It's the least I can do for him. I think it helps him too."

"Whatever you think is best." Mary took a short drink from the water jug. "I will be home before nightfall."

Mary traveled the long, dusty road until she reached the large Jordan River.

A crowd had already gathered along the banks listening to a man speak.

"Repent. The kingdom of heaven is near." Mary saw John standing near the river. His hair and clothes were covered in dirt. The garment he wore was little more than a camel's skin roughly cut to simply cover his bare flesh. It was cinched at his waist with a long piece of worn leather. His beard and hair were unkempt. He looked as if he had been traveling his whole life. "One is coming who was spoken of by the prophet Isaiah."

Mary watched as men walked toward the edge of the water where John stood.

"We wish to be baptized by you," one said.

"You brood of snakes! Who has warned you to flee from the coming wrath?" John's eyes grew large and his face turned red. "You need to bear fruit with repentance. Instead, you say to yourselves, 'We have Abraham as our father.' I tell you, God could raise up children from Abraham out of the stones at your feet. Even now the ax is laid to the root of the trees. Every tree that does not produce good fruit will be cut down and thrown into the fire."

The men murmured within their group.

John spoke even louder, addressing the crowd, "I baptize with water for repentance, but the one who is coming after me is greater than I. I'm not even worthy to carry his sandals like the lowest servant. He will baptize with the Holy Spirit and with fire. He will purge his threshing floor. He will gather his wheat into his storehouse, but he will burn the chaff with unquenchable fire."

Mary caught a disturbance in the crowd and watched the group part. A man walked through the open path and came near. His frame and build were strong, and somehow familiar. His eyes sparkled in the bright sunlight.

Jesus.

He passed her with a nod and a smile.

John recognized him too. "Look! The Lamb of God who takes away the sin of the world. This is the one who is coming."

"I wish to be baptized," Jesus said to John.

"Why have you come to me to be baptized when I need you to baptize me?"

"I need to be baptized. Please, John."

John waved to the water.

Mary watched Jesus follow him into the river.

John helped Jesus lower into the waters and be raised again.

When Jesus came up from the water, Mary noticed something land on him.

"What is that?" she asked.

"It looks like a dove," the woman beside her answered.

The bright blue sky thundered above them.

"It doesn't look like rain," another in the crowd remarked.

"This is my beloved son in whom I am well pleased," a voice echoed from above.

"What was that?" someone beside her asked.

"Was that thunder or an angel?" the first woman asked.

"I'm not sure. It sounded like a voice," Mary said. She made her way through the crowd when she saw Jesus leaving. "Wait," she called to him.

Jesus kept walking toward the desert.

"Mary?" John called to her.

She turned to face him. The dirt that had covered his face was now set to mud from the Jordan's water. She could see the deep lines in his skin and smell the stench of his worn clothes. "Yes."

"It is you. It has been some time."

"I enjoyed your message."

"It's not my message. It is from God."

"That was Jesus, wasn't it?" She pointed to the figure growing small in the distance.

"Yes. He is the one of whom I spoke."

"Where is he going?"

"He said he had important work to be done. I'm not sure exactly where he is heading."

Mary leaned up against her familiar wall just inside the gates of Jerusalem. The cool night air blew her hair around and refreshed her moist skin. It had been a hot day, but the sun was now set. This was her signal to begin her work. With another feast approaching, it would not be difficult to find wealthy travelers willing to part with a few coins. She would make their experience worth the expense.

"I'm telling you, I heard it true," a man was protesting to another. "That crazy man from the river was put in jail."

"It can't be true. John hasn't done anything wrong," the other argued as they passed Mary without a glance.

At the mention of John's name, Mary forgot her work to follow them and their conversation.

"It doesn't take much to anger Herod. Between all of John's babblings down by the river and his open rebuke of Herod's choice in taking Herodias as a wife, it doesn't surprise me that he is being held in chains."

"How long has he been there?"

"Months. Word is just now getting around.

Besides," the first continued. "John has been making trouble for the Pharisees, too. You know Herod is not going to let some madman ruin his chances at staying on Caesar's good side. If there was a revolt in Jerusalem, it would be Herod's head."

"Do you think Herod will be worried about John's followers revolting at his imprisonment?"

"I don't think he's got many left. I heard they started following another teacher."

"Who?"

"Some craftsman from Galilee."

"Everyone thinks they can be a teacher these days."

The two men rounded a corner, but Mary stopped in her tracks.

"A craftsman from Galilee. Jesus?" Mary wondered aloud. There was only one person who could answer her questions. She just hoped he would listen to the speech of a harlot this late at night.

Mary easily found her way through the streets of Jerusalem toward the large villa. Raising her headscarf from her shoulders to cover her hair, as was customary for the women of her people, she tucked in the last few strands before approaching the gate. She didn't want to take any chances of the strictly religious man having any reason to turn her away.

A guard approached on the other side of the gate and motioned her to halt.

"I'm called Mary," she spoke softly. "I've come to see Joseph."

"It's late." The muscular man looked her up and down. "Master has not called for a harlot."

"I'm a friend. Would you be so kind as to give him my name? Tell him Mary of Bethany has come to call."

The guard gave her a long look once more before he turned to march toward the house. It wasn't long before he returned. "You can wait in the garden," he said, opening the gate and pointing. "The master will be along shortly. Pray he doesn't ask me to dirty my sword with your blood. I just sharpened it."

Mary swallowed hard as she slid through the partially opened gate and around his tall frame.

He purposefully placed his hand on top of the hilt of his sword and pushed it around so the polished handle caught the moonlight.

She kept an eye on him over her shoulder until she found a bench in the garden.

The guard returned his attention to his appointed post.

A gentle gust brought different flower scents to Mary's nose and helped to relieve her fears. She knew Joseph would see her. Whether he would answer her questions was another matter.

Joseph originally came from Arimathea, but had made a home in Jerusalem many years ago when he was accepted onto the council. Mary's father had met Joseph in the Temple shortly after he moved to Jerusalem and the two became as close as brothers. Many family trips into the city included a stop at Joseph's villa. That was until her father died.

"Mary?" A man, whose tunic was disheveled from dressing quickly, came near to her. "Has something happened? Is Lazarus-"

"No," Mary stopped him with an up held hand. "All is well, my friend."

"Then why have you beckoned me from my bed at this hour?"

She rose to face him. "Is it true that John the Baptist has been taken into prison?"

"We could have talked about this in the morning," he said with apparent frustration in his voice. He gripped her elbow and turned her back to the front gate.

"Is it true?" She pulled away from him and dug her heels into the dirt.

He sighed and lowered himself onto the bench. "Yes. It is true."

"Why?" She sat on the edge of the bench.

"John has been causing Herod a lot of problems. He can't seem to keep his tongue from wagging."

"John only speaks truth."

"I know that," Joseph said, adjusting his tunic. "But he hasn't learned to hold his tongue when it could cost him his very life."

"What can be done?"

"Nothing. Herod has every right to hold John

for as long as he sees fit."

Mary kicked the sand.

"At least Herod has been lenient during John's captivity."

"What do you mean?"

"He's allowed John to have visitors. Word has it, his cousin has sent messengers back and forth."

Mary lifted her head. "Jesus?"

"Yes."

"I heard two men in the city talking about him. They called him a teacher."

"Anyone can call themselves a teacher," Joseph huffed. "Jesus has no formal training. He has spent the last three decades as a craftsman, not in the Temple learning from real teachers. I'd like to know under what authority he teaches."

Mary wondered herself.

"He's even got John's followers following after him like a young one after its mother."

"I heard that as well."

"Master." The guard from the gate ran up to the two of them. "Pardon the intrusion, but word has just arrived for you."

A messenger followed the guard.

"Speak," Joseph ordered. "I've already been interrupted this night."

"Word comes from Andrew and Peter," the young man began. His broad chest heaving up and down as he caught his breath.

At the sound of their names, Joseph and Mary rose from the bench at the same time.

"They sent me to tell you that John has been beheaded by Herod."

"What?"

"I speak truth."

"Speak on."

"Herod was entertaining for his birthday. Herodias' daughter was called to dance for him. Herod was so pleased by her that he offered to grant her any request, up to half his kingdom." He took a deep breath.

Joseph waved him on. "Well?"

"Upon consulting with her mother, she asked for the head of John the Baptist on a silver platter."

Mary sunk back down onto the bench and nearly missed it.

"And Herod agreed to this?"

"Yes. What else could he do in front of a room full of guests? He couldn't go back on his offer. I saw it for myself. John's bloody head was unveiled for all our eyes to see."

Mary's stomach turned over and she held her lips.

"Is that all?"

"Andrew and John have claimed the body and are preparing it for burial." The messenger bowed. "Any return word?"

"Not now." He waved the men away and returned to the bench.

Mary clutched her stomach.

"I don't know what is becoming of our great region." He looked over at her. "Do you need aid?"

She shook her head, but the motion made her feel nauseated. "I think I need to go home."

"Of course," he said, helping her to her feet. "Do you want my guard to go with you?"

"No." She took a deep breath of the fresh air and pushed away the unnerving thought of the guard following her home. "I'll be fine."

At The Festival Of Booths

"In the last day, that great day of the feast, Jesus stood and cried, saying, 'If any man thirst, let him come unto me, and drink.' "
-JOHN 7:37

One Month Later

Mary and Martha helped Lazarus into their booth.

"Sisters, you have done well. It looks wonderful."

The sisters beamed. They had constructed a simple stand and overlaid it with branches. Martha had hung dried fruit from the roof and the pleasant smell filled the small room.

Mary looked up and down the rows which made up the temporary town of booths that now lined the road outside of Jerusalem. She didn't care much for this particular festival, but knew how much it meant to Martha and Lazarus.

Martha adjusted a branch above Lazarus' head. "It will do."

"Greetings," a man called from a group heading toward their booth.

"Greetings, James," Mary kissed the man's cheeks.

"Martha!" Assia rushed to embrace the other sister.

"My dear friend. Are you well?" Martha asked, holding her at arm's length.

"Yes, I am well."

"Are all your siblings here?" Mary asked James.

"All but one," he answered, as his siblings gathered around him.

Mary tilted her head as she searched over the group. "Who have you left behind?"

"Jesus chose to stay in Galilee," Simon said.

"We told him to come and show himself," Judas offered. "He has been doing much good work."

"He said it wasn't his time. Whatever that is supposed to mean," Joseph replied.

"He's an adult and can choose for himself," Judas said.

"I agree, but if he intends to keep his followers, he needs to act. Instead, he hides at home," Joseph argued.

"Leave the matter alone. Let us enjoy the festival without him," Salome offered.

"Yes, please," Lydia said. "Your sisters have built a beautiful booth."

"It smells divine," Salome said, sniffing the air.

"Please," Martha waved into the booth. "Come and join us."

For the next three days, the seven siblings joined Mary and her family for the festival. The assembly of them went to the Temple and watched the traditions of their people unfold each day.

Early in the morning, a group of white-robed priests would walk down the well-worn stony path leading from the Temple to the pool of Siloam. One would carry a gold vessel which he used to draw water from the spring. As they ascended back to the Temple, musicians and every Jew who could travel followed the procession singing the songs of their ancestors.

The priest then took the water to the altar and walked a circle around it as the people shouted, "Hosanna!"

Being sure to stand on the western side, he poured the water out on the corner of the altar while another priest poured a drink offering out on the eastern side.

As the water ran down the brass, the priests shouted, "With joy, you will drink water out of the wells of salvation."

The people responded with the familiar words, "Praise the name of the Lord…"

Mary watched Lazarus and Martha chant along with the crowd. She saw the people waving bundles of branches. The sweet scent from the Etrog branches and the milder aroma from the Myrtle, Willow, and Palm branches were a welcomed change from the usual smell of blood and entrails on the altar. For that, Mary was deeply grateful.

During the hottest part of the third day, Mary and the other women were resting in the court of women.

"He is a good man," Salome said.

"I'm not saying our brother isn't a good man," Lydia replied. "I'm saying I believe Jesus deceives people." She pulled at her headpiece. "He says and does these impossible things. You know people are itching for someone to fulfill the promise that our lives will be better."

"I believe he speaks truth. And he's helped a lot of people. How can that be bad?"

"Helping people is not wrong, but He teaches contrary to our traditions."

Mary listened to the sisters while watching the people flow in and out of the open courtyard. When her eyes landed on a familiar figure, she rose without a word.

"Where are you going?" Martha called after her.

"I think I see Jesus," she answered over her shoulder.

The curious women followed her.

"Jesus? I thought he stayed behind," Lydia said, catching up to Mary.

"Me too," Assia agreed.

"He must have thought about what our brothers said and decided to join us," Salome said.

Jesus entered and sat in one of the rooms off

the court of women. A group of men surrounded him and another collection of men and women stood outside the opening listening in on the discussion.

"How does he know so much without being taught," a man asked.

Jesus faced him and answered, "I do not teach my own ways. Everything I say comes from the One who sent me. Anyone who wants to do God's will can know if my teaching is my own or God's. When people teach of their own thoughts, they do so for personal gain. When a man speaks only what the One who sent him tells him to speak, then that man speaks truth." He looked to the growing group of Pharisees. "Hasn't Moses given you the law? But none of you actually keep it. Why do you try to kill me?"

"Kill him?" Mary gasped.

"You are a madman," someone yelled from the group.

"He must be possessed by a demon," another said.

"No one is trying to kill you," a man sitting beside Jesus answered.

"I did one miracle and it amazed you all," Jesus said. "Yet, Moses gave you circumcision, even though it was given to the patriarchs before him." He glanced over at the Pharisees again. "You circumcise boys on the Sabbath. If you can legally do that, why are you angry at me for making a man's body whole on the Sabbath? Stop judging the outside of someone's actions."

"Is he the one the Pharisees tried to have killed when he healed that man's hand on the Sabbath?" a man near Mary asked. "He's here teaching again, but they are not doing anything. Do they believe him to be Messiah?"

Messiah? Mary stared at Jesus.

"But we know where he comes from," another answered. "When Messiah comes, we won't know where he is from."

"Yes," Jesus answered over the murmurings. "You know me. You know where I come from. I am not here teaching by my own authority. The One who sent me is true. You don't know him, but I know Him because I was with Him and then He sent me."

Some of the crowd dispersed with scoffs toward his madness.

"When Messiah comes, will he be able to perform more signs than this man?" a man asked the group.

"He has done many works," Salome added.

Mary watched the Pharisees call over a group of temple guards. The soldiers nodded to the men and then came towards the group.

Jesus said, "I will only be with you for a short time and I am going back to the One who sent me. You will try to find me, but you will not be able to find me. Where I will be, you can't come."

"I think the heat of the day has gotten to our brother," Assia whispered to Martha. "Perhaps we should take him somewhere to cool down."

"He speaks like a madman much more frequently," Lydia said. "I fear he is falling too ill to stay safe."

"Let's get him to our booth," Martha offered.

On the seventh morning of the festival, Mary watched the priest make seven circuits around the altar before pouring the water and drink offering out.

A commotion drew her attention away from the altar and she saw a familiar form coming near.

Jesus stood near and shouted over the clamor, "All who are thirsty come to me and I will give you drink."

"He is a prophet," a man yelled.

"He is Messiah," a woman called.

Two men argued beside Mary.

"Messiah can't be from Galilee," one said.

"Yes," the other answered. "Don't the prophecies tell us Messiah will come from David's line? From Bethlehem?"

Bethlehem. Mary bit her lip while she chewed on the idea. They knew of Jesus from Nazareth. Mary knew Jesus was actually born in Bethlehem. It was a curious thought.

"I think we need to get home," Martha said.

Mary nodded, not wanting her mouth to reveal

her inner thoughts.

At The Courtyard

"The teachers of the law and the Pharisees brought in a woman caught in adultery. They made her stand before the group."
-JOHN 8:3

The Day After The Festival

Mary opened her eyes to the sound of footsteps. She stirred.

"Shh," a voice soothed. "Go back to sleep, Mary."

"Jesus?" she whispered.

"Yes." He appeared in the doorway to her room.

"Has the sun risen?"

"No. It's still too early."

She pulled herself up onto her elbow. "Where are you going?"

"To pray and then to the Temple."

"Oh," she said and slid back to the ground.

"You should come to the Temple today."

"Why?"

"Trust me."

Mary went back to sleep until she heard Martha in the kitchen. She rose to help her sister with the morning chores before telling Martha, "I'm going to the Temple today."

Martha continued her work.

"Jesus is teaching today."

"Just send word if I have to feed half the town again." Martha didn't so much as look up at Mary.

"Yes, sister." Mary put on her headcloth and set out.

It was only a few hours before she made her way from Bethany, through the gates of Jerusalem and crowded streets, and finally found Jesus teaching in one of the side rooms of the court of women.

She stood nearby and listened to his words. At one point in his lesson, he caught her watching and nodded. She bowed her head and waved for him to continue. He spoke of many wonderful things that Mary thought only children and those will little hope should listen to, but she listened none the less.

A group of Pharisees rushed toward the room. Their exaggerated silk robes fluttering with their haste. One was dragging a woman by the arm.

Mary glanced at Jesus, who stood and watched them throw the woman at his feet.

"Teacher," the man spat the word. "This woman was captured in the very act of adultery."

Mary looked down to the woman on the ground. Her garment was tattered and barely clinging to her body. Her eyes were red from tears and her face was streaked with dust. Mary wanted very much to cover the young woman, but knew it was better to hold her instincts in front of the Pharisees. For she too might be caught in their hatred. She too had done enough to receive judgment from the law.

"The Law of Moses requires that we stone her," the apparent leader said. "But what do you say?"

Several of the men crossed their arms over their puffed-out chests. Others rubbed their well-oiled beards.

Jesus bent over and began writing in the sand with his fingers.

Mary stood up on her tiptoes, but couldn't see what he was writing over the group of men.

"Teacher?" the man spoke louder. "What do you say?"

Jesus straightened. "The man among you who is without any sin should cast the first stone," he said and bent down to continue writing.

Each man looked to others and then to the leader. The older man turned and walked away. One by one, the others followed without a word.

Jesus straightened again and glanced around. "Woman, where are your accusers?" He searched the courtyard. "Has no one condemned you?"

The woman lifted her head and looked around. "No one, Lord."

"Then neither do I condemn you," he said,

helping her rise. "Go your way and sin no more."

The woman bowed deeply and rushed down the giant steps.

Jesus turned to the group of listeners. "I am the light of the world," he said. "Anyone who follows me will not walk in darkness, but will have the light of life."

"You bear witness of yourself," one of the Pharisees who had turned back spoke. "And so, your witness is not true,"

"Even if I bear witness to myself, my witness is accurate," Jesus said. "I told you before, I know where I came from and where I am going. You don't know where I came from nor where I am going. You judge according to the outside, the flesh. I judge no one." He stepped forward. "And even if I did judge, my judgment would be true. I am not alone, but I am with the Father who sent me. Isn't written in your laws that the testimony of two men is all it takes to prove a fact?"

The man nodded.

"I bear witness to myself and the Father bears witness of me. That is two witnesses."

"Where is your father?" the man waved around the courtyard.

"You don't know me, nor my Father," Jesus answered. "If you knew me, you would know my Father too."

Mary took her time on the path from Jerusalem to Bethany. The events of the morning mingled with Jesus' words. She had seen this man as the infant who brought destruction and grief to her people. The events that took place since she was a child all seemed to revolve around Jesus' birth. He had been the root of all her hatred. He had been the reason for her pain. Yet, how could a man who provides nothing but healing be the target for all of her hate?

She heard people call him a demon-possessed madman. The religious leaders said he was trouble, but when Mary saw him forgiving the woman, he seemed saner and more peaceful than any man she had ever met. If he was lying, then how could he have more knowledge of God than any of the teachers combined? If he was controlled by a demon, then why would he bring restoration and forgiveness to souls? He told the woman to stop sinning. How could anyone but God forgive sins?

Questions filled her mind as she made her way down the familiar streets of Bethany toward her home. She might not have figured out everything Jesus was saying, but she knew in her heart she couldn't hate him anymore. Jesus spoke of forgiveness. The least she could do was forgive the infant who betrayed his people and the boy who chose stone and woodwork instead of overthrowing Roman rule. Besides, Jesus was just one man who was trying to do God's will.

Believing him and following his example of love couldn't change the world, right?

Mary stepped into the courtyard of her home.

"I'm glad you're back to help," Martha said from the kitchen.

"Forgive me, sister." Mary lowered her headpiece onto her shoulders. "I didn't mean to be gone so long."

"Well, get started on slicing the fruit. They should be here soon."

Mary shook her foggy head. "They?"

"Lazarus invited Jesus and his disciples to our house for the evening meal. They sent word earlier that they would be arriving before nightfall. Of course, you know those poor men cannot go anywhere without having a crowd follow them." Martha began to pace about and pick up things around the courtyard. "If those people think I am going to feed every James and John that gather in our town simply because-"

"Jesus is coming?" Mary went to the entrance.

"Mary, honestly?" Martha clicked her tongue. "Can you focus for just a moment, please?"

Mary looked back at her sister and then down at the floor. "Sorry."

"That's better."

Mary didn't look up, but she didn't need to do so to know that Martha had lifted her chin ever so slightly in victory.

"As I was saying, we need to get the house ready for the guests. They will be here shortly,"

Martha continued speaking as she fussed about the room deciding what needed to be done.

All of Martha's words fell on deaf ears as Mary thought about Jesus walking into her home and sitting in the very room in which she was standing. She had witnessed his kindness and gentleness to the adulterous woman that morning.

She tried to imagine where he would settle and what he would teach about this time. Maybe he would want to be somewhere by the door and window so that the people who stood outside could hear him. She pulled herself up on her toes to look out the high window and waited to see a glimpse of his coming.

When she finally saw the dust of the street begin to stir, she knew a large crowd of people was headed her way and somewhere among them would be Jesus. She ran to find Martha.

"Martha, Martha, they are heading this way."

Martha took one last look over the room. Then she ran out the front door and down the street to meet Jesus and his followers.

Mary stayed at the window, watching and waiting.

As the crowd drew close to the house, Mary could hear Martha speaking to Jesus, "...such an honor to have you in our home. My brother will be along shortly."

The large group of men followed Martha into the house and began to make themselves comfortable around the open courtyard.

Mary caught a glimpse of Jesus through the crowd. For just a moment, she was able to catch his glance before he was pulled away by one of his disciples. She couldn't be sure, but she thought he smiled at her. He always seemed to be smiling and it was contagious as she fought a losing battle to hide the one that had found its way to her pink lips.

She floated about the room in order to make her way closer to Jesus, who had found a spot in the center to sit.

As soon as Jesus began speaking, the entire room fell silent and all focus was turned toward him. His voice was almost musical in its tone that it sounded more like a chant, yet masculine enough to demand any person's full attention.

Mary found herself close enough that she could almost reach out and touch Jesus' toes. Listening to his words, she was mesmerized. She hung on every word that dripped out of his mouth like honey. She smiled and nodded as he expounded on the scriptures she had heard since she was little, but they were delivered unlike any teacher she had ever heard.

Unaware of just how long she had been sitting, Mary noticed Martha walk by her with a plate of fruit and offered it to Jesus before giving her a nasty look and returning to the kitchen. Mary stretched her shoulders and adjusted her position.

A few moments later, Martha was back at Jesus' side again trying to offer him more food and drink as he taught.

As he turned her down for the second time, Martha huffed and interrupted the lesson, "Lord, don't you care that my sister has left me to serve alone?" She looked down at Mary and then back at Jesus before moving the tray of food to her hip. "Make her come help me." Martha waved her free hand in her sister's direction and then placed it on her other hip.

Jesus looked up at her. "Martha, Martha." He shook his head slightly. "You are vigilant and troubled about many things, but only one thing is needed. Mary has chosen the good thing and it will not be taken away from her."

Martha huffed and stormed out of the room without apologizing to those in her way.

Mary cringed as she watched her sister's body disappear into the kitchen. She shuttered at the thought of whoever would cross Martha's path first. They would certainly get the fullness of her wrath.

When Mary turned back, she met eyes with Jesus. She expected to feel shame or, at the very least, embarrassment in his gaze. Instead, she felt a wash of acceptance and love bathe her soul. This man was different and she was beginning to enjoy being in his presence.

As the sun was setting and the crowd left to go to their own homes, Martha found Mary. "I've invited Jesus and his followers to stay the night," she said.

"Yes, of course."

"They have a long way to travel and I thought it would be good for them to have rest before they leave."

Later, Mary stood in the open courtyard of her home listening to the sounds of life. Martha had finished a grand feast and was serving it in the upper room. Mary perked up when she heard someone coming down the ladder.

"Mary," Jesus said, stepping into the courtyard from the last step of the ladder.

"Yes?"

"Why aren't you up there with the rest?"

Mary smiled. "I just needed some fresh air. It's good to have so many friends in one room. It can just be a little overwhelming when one is not used to it."

Jesus nodded. "Did you enjoy the festival?"

"Yes. It was nice to get away from Bethany and see old friends again."

"You don't make it to the Temple often?"

Mary shook her head and looked down. "A woman of my..." She tripped over her words. "...profession isn't exactly welcomed with open arms in the Temple. I try to make the festivals where I can blend in some, but I don't go as much as Martha and Lazarus would like me to."

The Temple was supposed to be the place where God resided with His people," Jesus said, as he leaned his elbow on the ladder. "Yet, those people have turned it into a place of judgment and gain. They are not doing what was instructed of them. The Temple was supposed to be a place where all were to be welcomed to meet with God. Not a guild for those with the stiffest necks and largest money pouches." He stretched out his neck and held up an imaginary money purse.

Mary chuckled.

Jesus relaxed. "It's good to hear you laugh."

Laughter from the upper room cascaded down on them.

"It's good to hear laughter in this home too. It doesn't come as often as it should."

"I'm glad your brother is doing well."

Mary looked toward the upper room. She could picture Lazarus reclined at the head of the table, stuffing his face full of the delicious food and it caused her to smile. "Me too."

Jesus put his hands on one of the rungs of the ladder. "Care to join us?"

"In a moment."

Jesus put a foot on the step.

"Actually," Mary said. "There is something I wanted to show you while you were here."

Jesus stepped off the ladder. "Lead on."

A few moments later, Mary was opening a gate to a large vineyard close to the Mount of Olives.

"I had to sell this vineyard after Father died, but I was able to buy it back recently. I know the leaders are not happy with you." She wandered around the garden, picking dead leaves off the vines. "I know my parents loved you like one of their own. Father bought this garden for Mother. If you ever need a place to hide, a refuge from the raging storm turning against you, I want you to know you are welcome here."

"That's very gracious of you."

"I'm trying to tend to it so it will turn a profit for our family." She stopped to inspect a young branch. "Maybe if I can care for it enough, I can leave my...current profession." She looked up to see Jesus' face close to hers. The nearness of him made the heat rise in her cheeks. She cleared her throat and continued to walk. "It's an extensive vineyard and it's hidden from the main road. It can be a very private place to think."

"Or pray."

"I suppose," she thought. "If one believed God was still listening."

At The Gate

"My sheep listen to my voice; I know them, and they follow me."
-JOHN 10:27

Three Months Later, Feast of Dedication

Mary stood in the court of women, half listening to Jesus teach and half watching the crowds. This had become her routine whenever Jesus was in Jerusalem. She would come to the Temple to hear him teach and he would often stay at her home with his followers when the sun went down. She had given up working the streets of Jerusalem at night and spent much of her time working her vineyard. It was harder work, but at least she could feel some honor in it.

She watched a shepherd lead a large group of sheep through the Sheep Gate on the eastern wall. Even with forgiveness in her soul, she had to look away at the sheep being brought to the Temple. She had been taught that they were a sacrifice, but she knew they had no choice. The innocent animals would follow the lead of their shepherd.

Even if it meant leading them to their deaths.

Her face was hidden under her headcloth until she met eyes with Jesus.

He nodded and said, "I tell you the truth, the thief and robber does not enter the fold by the door, but by climbing in another way." He held her eyes. "But the one who enters by the door is the shepherd of the sheep. The doorkeeper opens the door for the shepherd. He calls the sheep by name so they will follow him. They will not follow strangers because they don't know their voice. All who came before me were strangers, thieves, and robbers who the sheep would not listen to." Jesus turned to the crowd that was listening to him. "I am the door. If anyone enters through me, he will be saved. I will lead them out and bring them to good pasture. The thief comes to steal, kill, and destroy, but I have come to bring abundant life." He glanced back at Mary. "I am the good shepherd. A good shepherd would lay down his life for his sheep. Unlike a hired hand, who runs if a wolf comes to devour the sheep."

Mary's heart raced as she held his gaze.

"I am the good shepherd." He pointed to his chest. "I know my own sheep and they know me. I will lay down my life for my sheep." He looked over the group of faces before continuing, "I have other sheep as well. I must bring them in too. They will hear my voice and will become one with my flock and with me. This is the reason my Father loves me, because I lay down my life and I will take it up again."

Lay down my life. The words echoed in Mary's mind.

"No one," Jesus interrupted her thoughts with a deep voice. "No one can take my life away from me, but I lay it down by my own choice. I have the power to lay it down and I have the power to take it up again, all by the command of my Father."

"When are you going to tell us the truth?" A man yelled from across the way.

Mary turned to see a group of Pharisees charging toward Jesus.

"If you really are Messiah, then come right out and tell us," the leader continued as he stormed through the crowd and met Jesus face to face.

"I told you and you didn't believe me," Jesus said with all the calmness of the Dead Sea on a windless day. "Everything that I do in my Father's name is a record and testimony of myself. You don't believe because you are not my sheep. As I said, 'My sheep hear my voice. I know them and they follow me.' I gave them eternal life and they will never die. No one will snatch them out of my hand." He held out one hand and then closed it. "My Father is greater than everyone and He gave them to me. No one can snatch them out of His hand." Jesus put his other hand over his fist. "I and my Father are one."

"Blasphemer!" the lead Pharisee exclaimed.

Mary watched each man pull a large stone from under his robe and lift it high in the air.

"I have shown you many good works from my Father. For which one do you stone me?" Jesus demanded.

"We are not going to stone you for good works, but for your blasphemy. You try to make yourself equal with God when you are only a man."

Jesus shook his head. "Doesn't your own law say, 'you are gods'? If the prophet spoke God's words, then how can I be blaspheming when the Father told me what to say? If I don't do my Father's works, then don't believe me. If I do, then, even if you don't believe me, at least believe the works so that you can believe that my Father and I are one."

Mary saw the man's face turn bright red as he raised his stone above his head. She turned to where Jesus was teaching, but he was no longer there. The crowd rushed around in chaos as Mary searched for him.

When the area had been cleared by the Temple guards, Mary couldn't find Jesus anywhere. She decided to go home to tell Martha and Lazarus all that had happened.

On her walk to Bethany, she thought on all Jesus had said.

A shepherd passed her with his small flock.

I am the good shepherd. My sheep hear my voice and follow it. Jesus' voice resonated in her mind.

Mary stopped to watch the animals follow the

man with the staff in his hand.

I lay my life down for my sheep.

A lump caught in her throat.

No one can take my life, but I lay it down willingly.

She held her hands to her trembling lips. *He is not going to overthrow Rome like his disciples say. He's going to sacrifice himself.*

Picking up the hem of her dress, Mary rushed to her home to share the message with Martha. She wanted nothing more than to speak with Jesus, but she had no idea where to look for him. At least Martha would listen to her words.

At The Bedside

"Now a certain man was sick, named Lazarus, of Bethany, the town of Mary and her sister Martha."
-JOHN 11:1

One Month Later

Mary made her way softly into her brother's room, hoping her footsteps would not wake him if he were sleeping. This was the second day he stayed in his room when he should have been up. Martha had said it was nothing to worry about, but Mary had watched Lazarus' health slowly fade over the past few weeks. They had tried every medicine mixture they could find, but nothing seemed to help.

Moving the sheer curtain away, Mary carefully entered the dim room and placed the tray she had been carrying down on the floor beside his bedroll. As she turned around to leave, she saw Lazarus' body stir out of the corner of her eye.

"Mary?" he whispered.

"I'm right here," she said, grabbing his

extended hand carefully. It looked pale and fragile enough to be broken by even a weak creature such as herself.

She heard a noise rise in his throat as he tried to speak, "Mary."

"Shh, it's all right. I'm right here, dear brother. Take it easy." She gently brushed away some of the dark hair that stuck to her brother's sweaty brow.

"Mary," he said before she watched his bloodshot eyes roll back and his dry mouth gasp for another breath.

"Shh, rest now, brother." She wiped his brow with a wet cloth she had brought on the tray and then kissed his head.

Mary crept out of the room with a short glance back over her shoulder. Making her way into the kitchen, she found Martha. "Martha?" she whispered.

"Yes?" Her sister answered without turning around.

"Lazarus is getting worse."

She watched the arm that Martha was using to cut up a pomegranate stop in mid chop and her head fall slightly. "I know."

"Isn't there anything else we can do?"

Martha continued cutting as she shook her head. "I don't think so."

Mary began to walk away to go check on Lazarus again when she heard Martha say, "Unless..."

Turning back toward her, Mary asked, "Unless what?"

Martha lifted her head and looked at the stone wall as if in some kind of trance.

"Martha?" Mary begged. "What is it?"

"Jesus." His name fell softly from Martha's lips.

Mary held her hands to her stomach as if she had been hit there. "Jesus. What made you think of him?"

"I heard he was close by. Lazarus spoke of having him over again," Martha said as she turned her head just enough towards Mary to show that a slight smile had crept across her lips before it disappeared. "We could send for him. We've seen him heal before. I'm sure he would come for Lazarus."

Mary's stomach jumped into her throat. "He has healed before," she whispered so quietly that she wasn't sure if Martha hadn't heard her or was just ignoring her.

Martha wiped her hands on a nearby rag. "I can find a messenger." She rushed out of the room.

Mary sat staring at her brother through the doorway of his room. "Hold on." She reached down and squeezed his hand.

When Martha came back, her face was flushed. "It's done. I sent word," she said through short breaths.

"Do you think he will come?"

"I don't know." Martha shrugged. "He does care very much for our brother, but I don't know."

Mary bowed her head and began to pray out loud, "God, please help my brother. Send Jesus to us with much haste to spare my brother's life. We need him."

The sisters spent the rest of the day sitting beside their brother listening for the sound of footsteps. They watched every breath enter and leave Lazarus' body. He gasped several times making them think it was the last time they would watch a breath leave his lips, but then he would take one more.

"He's holding on," Martha said, as a tear rolled down her cheek.

"For what?" Mary asked.

"I'm not sure."

Mary leaned down and whispered into Lazarus' ear, "It's all right, brother. Go in peace. We love you. Rest now, sweet brother."

Martha began to weep. She leaned over and whispered into his other ear, "Yes. Go now, brother. Your sisters will be well."

Lazarus tried desperately to smile and say something, but his dry mouth sucked the life out of the expression.

Mary saw her brother's eyes roll up and a single tear run down his face and fall onto the bedroll.

The two sisters watched through tears as Lazarus took one last deep breath and then the air slowly left his body. Both held their breath as they waited for their brother to take another one. He did not. As the moments passed, both realized he was gone in the same moment.

Mary heaved and laid across his body as she let the sadness she had been holding back release with full force.

Martha let her breath out with a loud sigh and then joined her sister across their brother's body.

"He's gone!" Mary screamed and buried her face in Lazarus' chest.

Martha sat up and stroked Mary's hair.

Mary looked down at the body under her. Seeing the empty eyes of her brother staring back at her, she slowly reached up and forced his eyelids closed.

"Peace, dear brother," she whispered through small sobs. "I do hope you have found peace."

At The Door

> *"Therefore his sisters sent unto him, saying, 'Lord, behold, he whom thou lovest is sick.' "*
> -JOHN 11:3

The Next Morning

Mary sat in the open courtyard staring at the front door. When a shadow covered the light pouring in, Mary lifted her head to see the messenger standing before her.

He ran up to her and bowed. "Jesus sends this message, 'This sickness will not end in death. It is for God's glory. So that God's Son may be glorified through it.'"

Mary's tears filled her eyes afresh. "Where is He?"

"He did not follow."

"He's not coming?" Mary asked as she rose on her wobbly feet.

"He did not say."

Mary scrunched her forehead in frustration.

"Jesus is not coming?" Martha asked as she entered the room.

Mary shook her head.

The messenger looked back and forth between the two women.

Martha waved him off and stepped back into the kitchen.

Mary rushed after her. "What does this mean?"

"I don't know. I thought..." She wiped her hands on her dress to remove wrinkles that were not there. "...I thought he would come." The words choked in her throat.

"I thought he would have come too."

"I'll start the preparations," Martha said. "When the town hears about Lazarus' death, there will be many people coming to-"

"Is that all you care about?" Mary yelled.

Martha looked down with pain on her face.

Realizing she had wounded her, Mary sighed deeply. "Oh, sister. I am so sorry. Forgive me. I didn't mean-"

Martha held up her hand. "I know what you meant. I'll handle the preparations. You take all the time you need to grieve." She turned away from her.

"Martha, I'm sorry. Please don't-"

Pausing, Martha turned over her shoulder and shook her head. "I'm fine. We all grieve in different ways. I need to remember that and you need to learn it." Then she turned back and walked into the kitchen.

Mary went to Lazarus' room. Martha had

covered his body with a clean linen. Mary laid down next to her brother's body and let the tears continue to flow from her eyes. She heard the familiar sounds of preparation in their home.

For the rest of the day, people came in and out of the room as Mary laid on the floor. Noises and bodies became a blur as the weight of grief covered her. She could do nothing more than breathe and even that became difficult.

Martha rushed around catering to the mass of people who filled her home to mourn for Lazarus. It seemed as if everyone in Bethany and most of the surrounding cities had piled into the stone house.

Once things had settled down and everyone had their time of visitation, Martha came into the room where Mary was still laying on the floor.

"Mary," Martha called, as she knelt beside her.

Mary rolled onto her back to look up into her sister's eyes.

"Mary," Martha said, as she brushed some hair away from her face. "It's time."

New tears formed in Mary's eyes. "But he has not come yet."

Martha took a deep breath and held her sister's quivering chin with her palm. "I... I don't think he's coming, sister."

Closing her eyes tight, Mary prayed with all her heart. "He will come. I know he will."

"Mary, we can't wait any longer to-"

"He will come." Mary interrupted.

Martha sighed and then sucked in a deep breath. "We cannot wait any longer. We need to prepare the body for burial. I'm sure whatever has kept Jesus from coming was important and-"

"More important than his best friend?" Mary begged.

Martha shook her head and looked to the side.

"More important than us?"

Martha shook her head again. "I don't know. I'm hurt just like you, but we can't keep Lazarus in the house until Jesus decides if he will come. He is very busy."

Mary rolled over to her side to face her brother's body again, putting her back to Martha. "Why won't he just come? Why didn't he come when we called him? He could have healed Lazarus."

Martha rubbed her arm. "I don't have answers. Like you, I only have questions."

Mary began to sob again when Martha left.

When she returned, Martha had a tray full of bottles and pieces of linens.

Sitting up, Mary looked at her.

"Do you want to help?" Martha asked.

Mary nodded and wiped her face with the back of her hand.

They worked together to undress and wipe Lazarus' body clean. Afterward, Mary began to prepare the strips by rubbing spices into the linen and setting them into a small pile. While Martha rubbed some mixes all over their brother's body and then carefully placed the strips one at a time over the flesh.

Fragrances filled the entire house.

Mary caught the scent of Spikenard. "That was Mother's favorite."

"No wonder Father kept so much of it."

Martha saw the light in Mary's eyes and tilted her head.

"I was just thinking that these are the spices Lazarus would have picked out for himself," Mary answered the unasked question on Martha's face. "He would have wanted to remember Mother too."

Martha nodded and looked over the trays. "I guessed he would have wanted the best. It's a good thing we haven't sold off the entire supply yet."

It was Mary's turn to nod.

"That should be enough," Martha said as Mary placed another strip in the pile. "Help me lift his leg."

Mary did as she was asked.

The sisters finished wrapping Lazarus' body up to his shoulders.

Mary reached for the folded piece of cloth on the tray. "His prayer cloth," she said, as she rubbed the material between her fingers. "I remember when Father was trying to teach Lazarus to pray. He was so stubborn and he got mad every time he couldn't remember the right words."

"I remember," Martha agreed.

Mary rubbed the cloth once more and then laid it delicately over Lazarus' eyes.

They carefully wrapped his head with a sheer cloth. When they were done, Martha removed the tray. She came back into the room and sat on the opposite side of the body from Mary. "It's getting late. Some of the men are waiting to carry him to the tomb before dark."

Mary wiped more tears away. "Very well."

The sisters followed the men with most of the small town of Bethany crying behind them.

Once the crowd got to the cave, men had already rolled away the massive stone and lit some of the torches so the family could enter.

The mourners' cries echoed off the mountain and seemed to go on forever. The sea of black and sackcloth reminded Mary of the day they had buried their father, and their mother before him. Even some of the faces were the same, except weathered by time and the elements.

Martha and Mary followed the men as they carried their brother deep into the dark cave.

After placing the body on one of the shelves, the men left the two sisters alone.

Martha glanced at the decaying bodies of their parents and other relatives that were buried in the family tomb. "How many more?" She whispered.

Mary didn't answer. She knew the two of them were the last remaining members of their family. Mary shuddered at the thought of either Martha having to bury Mary or herself having to stand over her sister's body.

"Peace, brother," Martha said, as she caressed his wrapped head.

Mary hugged herself more against the grief that filled her heart than the cool air of the cave.

They walked back into the light and watched the men roll the large stone back in front of the mouth of the cave.

Mary jumped at the sound of the round boulder landing in its place in the hewn rock.

Martha invited the crowd back to their home for food.

Mary stayed watching the stone until it was too dark to see her hand in front of her face. Then she pulled herself away and headed toward home. Alone.

The next two days were seen through tears as Mary mourned the loss of her brother.

Martha spent her time trying to clean things that didn't need to be cleaned or move things around three or four times. Even with a large number of women who came to stay with them while they grieved, Martha found work to do. The women kept delicious aromas pouring from the kitchen.

When Mary found the strength to climb off her straw mat, she found herself sitting on the floor in the courtyard simply staring at the place where Jesus had sat. Her soul was plagued with the same question as she turned it over and over in her mind. *Why didn't He come?*

New faces and old faces mingled together in a blur of olive skin and dark hair. None of them was the face Mary wanted to see. She stared at the place in the freshly swept stone floor and tried to imagine Jesus sitting there telling a parable. Mary missed him. She missed Lazarus. She missed her parents. The tears came again and Mary buried her head in her drawn-up knees.

She felt a hand pat her head and rub her right shoulder.

"Poor thing," a familiar female voice said. "She is so saddened by her brother's passing."

Another voice whispered nearby, "Yes, poor dear. I wish there were more we could do for her."

"What more can be done?" The first asked. "All of Bethany has turned out for them and half the city of Jerusalem."

"Lazarus was so loved."

The first voice hummed in agreement while she brushed down some of Mary's hair back into her covering as a mother would do to her daughter.

Mary missed her own mother. Her body heaved with fresh sobs.

More people came and went as the house was alive with activity. Some would come and sit with Mary while others made themselves useful helping

Martha in the kitchen.

Mary wanted to help too. She wanted to get up and go about her chores to show everyone that she was well, but her body hurt so much with a deep ache that started on the inside and made its way through every part of her. It hurt to move. It hurt to cry. It hurt to even think.

As she sat still with her head on her knees, she heard someone call from the front entrance. She looked up just in time to see a messenger run toward the kitchen. His cheeks were so flushed it looked like he had been running all day. Mary put her chin back down on her knees while she found the spot on the floor that she had been staring at before the interruption.

Rushing legs flew past her as she glanced to see Martha running out the doorway behind the man. Mary closed her eyes and could hear the footsteps on the hard earth.

Voices murmured all around her for several moments.

Suddenly, Martha appeared and crouched down next to her. She wiped some loose hair away from her sister's glazed eyes and whispered, "He has come and is calling for you."

Looking up into Martha's dark brown eyes, Mary blinked a few times before she understood what she was saying. When she did, Mary got up and ran out of the house.

As Mary rushed outside in the blinding sun, she heard several of the mourners calling after her,

"Look, she is going to the grave to weep there."

Mary put her hand over her eyes to block the bright sun as she saw his face just a stone's throw away. She began to run, but tripped over herself and ended up falling down at his feet. She bowed her head to the hot, sandy ground and said the one thing that had consumed her thoughts for the past few days, "Lord, if you had been here, my brother would not have died."

Allowing the fiery tears to flow freely, Mary looked up into his face.

Jesus bent down and cupped her shaking chin. He wiped her face gently with his thumb and gazed into her eyes. "Where have you laid him?" He asked softly.

Pulling herself up as he rose, Mary said, "Lord, come and see." Waving him toward the direction of the family's burial cave, she picked up the hem of her dress and began to walk.

Jesus didn't move as Mary took a few steps away, so she walked back to Him. Searching his face, she noticed tear lines streaked down his dusty cheeks. Her heart skipped a beat and she could see his face soften.

Jesus reached his hand out and cupped the side of her face.

Mary rubbed her cheek deep into his rough palm and closed her eyes. She breathed in his sweet, earthy smell and held onto it. It was almost intoxicating as it sent a deep wave of calmness crashing over her aching body.

She heard someone behind her say, "Look at how he loved Lazarus!"

Jesus pulled his hand slowly away from her face and Mary looked around to see the crowd which had filled her house was now surrounding them.

An older man said, "He opened the eyes of the blind, couldn't he have healed this man?"

Glancing back at Jesus, Mary tilted her head as he wiped away the wetness from his face. He nodded at her and then looked in the direction of the mountain. Mary headed in that direction and he kept right by her side as they made their way to the place where Lazarus was buried.

Once they came upon the cave, Mary noticed the large crowd of sackcloth had followed them. She found Martha in the crowd and waved her sister to join them.

Jesus had his eyes focused on the large stone that blocked the opening to the cave.

Without looking at anyone in particular, Jesus said, "Take away the stone."

Gasps echoed off the mountain, but no one moved.

Martha leaned over to Jesus and whispered, "Lord, by this time he stinks. He has been dead four days."

Mary watched as Jesus turned toward Martha and looked her right in the eyes. He said, "Didn't I tell you that, if you would believe, you should see the glory of God?"

Martha nodded and then found two large men

in the crowd. "Do as he says," she ordered.

Sharing a slight glance of uncertainty, the two men walked over to the large boulder and carefully pushed it away until the mouth of the cave was open before them.

Jesus stepped closer as Mary saw many around them take a step backward. He lifted his eyes up to the clear blue sky and said, "Father, I thank you that you have heard me and I know that you always hear me, but because of the people which stand by I said it, that they may believe that you have sent me." Then he looked into the dark cave and cried with a loud voice, "Lazarus, come out!"

Mary heard many whispers race through the crowd like lightning. She kept her eyes on Jesus' back as he stared into the dark cave.

After a few moments, Mary rubbed her eyes and blinked a few times. She thought she was dreaming. A form was slowly moving in the darkness toward the light. When it made its way out of the cave, she took a cautious step closer.

"Lazarus," the word slipped from her lips as she began to tremble.

Martha gasped behind her.

The body of their brother was taking small steps toward them, but the burial clothes were inhibiting his movements.

Jesus turned to a few men standing near and said to them, "Loose him and let him go."

They nodded and rushed to Lazarus.

Watching them pull away the strips, Mary was

not sure what to expect. Her mind imagined her brother's flesh had begun to rot and she cringed as the linens fell to the ground. She wanted to look away, but couldn't. She wanted even more to see life in her brother's eyes again.

When they had removed the last piece of cloth, Mary looked on the unmarked flesh of Lazarus. She was shocked. He looked even better than the last time she saw him. The fever had taken over his body, causing his medium olive skin to turn white and his eyes had shifted from white to the color of blood. Mary remembered all the days she had taken care of the sick little boy. Lazarus stood before all of them as if he had never been ill a day in his life, much less had been dead for four days. His olive skin looked perfectly toasted and his eyes were the brightest white Mary had ever seen.

She pulled her clasped hands toward her chest and looked over at Jesus. "Thank you," she mouthed.

He nodded quietly and then disappeared into the crowd.

Walking over to her brother, Mary reached up and touched his face. "Oh, Lazarus," she cried.

"Greetings, sweet sister," he laughed.

Mary wrapped her arms tightly around her brother's neck.

In a moment, they were joined by Martha who was wrapping her arms around both of them.

The crowd cheered and came to embrace the dead man who walked again among the living.

"What do you mean, you're leaving?" Mary wept.

"I can't stay here," Jesus said. "It's no longer safe for me."

The night was cool and Mary had suggested they take a walk in her vineyard. She needed to get away from the full house and massive celebration of Lazarus' return from the dead. She loved her brother and was glad to have him back, but the crowd pressed in on her and she needed to breathe. Jesus had gladly accepted the invitation for some fresh air and a walk in the starlit night.

"You can stay here." She stepped toward him. "You can stay with me." Mary reached for Jesus' hand and placed his palm on her wet cheek. "Please?"

"Mary…" He held her face. "I can't. It's not my time yet."

At The House

"Then Jesus six days before the passover came to Bethany, where Lazarus was which had been dead, whom he raised from the dead."
-JOHN 12:1

Two Months Later, Friday Evening

Mary stood at the kitchen table chopping root vegetables for the evening meal.

Martha was humming to herself in the courtyard as she sewed a stitch in a torn dress.

Lazarus was in the back of the house, tending to their small garden.

Martha put the dress down on her lap and sighed.

"Are you well, sister?" Mary asked.

"Oh yes. I was just thinking about how wonderful life is when one doesn't have to worry about someone getting sick."

Mary nodded in agreement. "Lazarus' hasn't fallen ill since we got him back."

"No. Rather the opposite. For the past two months, he has strutted around here like a prized ram sent out in the pasture to stud. He's been working like he's making up for the last several decades I had to lead this house.

Mary chuckled. "Oh, sister. You know you'd do it all over again."

"Of course," Martha said with a short huff. "He is our brother. I wouldn't have changed anything about it." She picked up her sewing. "Though it is nice to have him healthy."

"Yes. Maybe now you can lighten up on your housework." Mary tossed a slice of radish at her.

"Mary!" Martha shouted as the food landed beside her.

Mary broke out into a long belly laugh.

"You pick that up right now," the younger sister demanded.

Mary tossed another piece of radish at Martha and it landed in her hair.

"Mary!"

Tears blurred Mary's eyes and she had to hold her stomach from all the laughter.

Martha stood and reached for her broom. She chased after Mary. "You clean that up or I'll-"

"Or what?" Mary said, dodging a swat from the broom.

"Mary," a deep voice called from the doorway.

Mary turned to see him. "Jesus." She rushed to embrace him. "It's been months with no word. Are you well?" She pulled him back to arm's length to look at him. His face was worn and tanned by the sun. His clothes were dirty from weeks without being cleaned.

Martha came to stand next to them. "Master, have you come to teach my sister another lesson?"

"It looks as though you were doing well teaching her on your own," he said, eyeing the broom in her hand.

Martha blushed and hid the broom behind her back. She looked over his shoulder. "I see you're not alone."

Mary looked around him to the group of men coming up to the house.

"I'll get some food ready," Martha said, walking into the kitchen.

Mary looked up into his tired eyes. "Please, come sit."

Jesus entered the house and sat in his usual place in the open courtyard.

"We've been all over," Peter said, walking in the door. "It will be good to rest."

"Yes," Mary said to the men, showing each of them into her home. "Come in and dine with us. Tomorrow is the Sabbath and you will have your rest with us."

Once everyone was gathered, Mary found a place near Jesus. "Will you stay with us for the coming Passover?"

Jesus swallowed hard and lowered the bowl in his hands.

"I know you have a lot of places to visit, but it would be nice to have you and your followers stay. At least until after the festival."

"I don't know if we would be welcomed in Jerusalem," James said with a mouthful of stew.

"I'm waiting for the time we walk into the city and seize it for ourselves," Simon said.

"Yes," John agreed.

"There will be no more of that talk," Jesus corrected them. "We are all tired from our journey." He looked at Mary. "We shall stay for as long as we can. And we are grateful for the hospitality."

At The Entry

"...behold, thy King cometh unto thee: he is just, and having salvation; lowly, and riding upon an ass, and upon a colt the foal of an ass."
-ZECHARIAH 9:9

Monday Morning

"Mary, I need you to go to the Temple and pick out the lambs," Martha said.

"Martha, you know I can't-"

"I have too much to do today to go." Martha waved around the kitchen. "Take Mary Magdalene with you."

Mary fought down the waves crashing in her stomach and went to search out her friend. She found her behind the house with some of the other women who had followed Jesus to Bethany.

"Mary," the group called.

"Greetings," Mary said.

"Thank you for allowing us to visit while Jesus and his disciples are staying with you," Mary of Nazareth said.

"I love having you in my home, Mother." Mary

did enjoy the older woman's company. She reminded her of her own mother and always carried a gentle spirit. Mary thought of the devotion she had for her son. Wherever Jesus seemed to go, he was not only followed by the group of men he taught, but also by a small group of women who financially supported them. Mary of Nazareth, his mother, led the women. Mary Magdalene had joined them when they visited her region on one of his trips. Jesus' Aunt Mary, his father's sister, had recently joined Mary of Nazareth to look after the older woman. Joanna and Susanna rounded out the group.

Joanna was a young widow. Her husband had died all too young, but left her with a comfortable living. When Jesus taught in Galilee, she decided to use her husband's fortune to provide for the needs of the men. Susanna was younger and had lost many family members to illnesses. Nothing much tied her to Galilee and the idea of following a traveling Rabbi gave meaning to her life. The six women followed Jesus and his disciples everywhere. They prepared meals, mended garments, and were available for any need that arose.

Mary stood before all their bright faces. "I'm glad to have the company. Mary Magdalene, may I speak to you a moment?"

"Of course," the woman excused herself from the group.

"I need to go to the Temple. Will you join

me?"

"Are you picking out the lambs?"

"Yes."

As the two women walked the path toward Jerusalem, Mary spotted Jesus and his followers standing by the Mount of Olives. They made their way to stand nearby and hear what the men were saying.

"John," Jesus beckoned. "Go with Peter into the city. There you will find a donkey tied up with her colt. Untie both of them and bring them here to me. If anyone says anything to you about taking the animals, tell them, 'The Lord has need of them.'"

The two men ran off to obey Jesus' instructions.

"What do you think he needs with two donkeys?" Mary Magdalene asked Mary.

"I am not sure, but it does remind me of something."

"What?"

Mary closed her eyes and repeated the saying she remembered from childhood, "The prophet Zechariah said, 'Rejoice greatly, oh daughter of Zion. Shout, oh daughter of Jerusalem. Behold, your King comes unto you. He is just, and has salvation, lowly and riding upon a colt of a donkey.'"

"But that only says he will come riding on the colt."

Mary nodded. "What better way to break a

young colt than to have its mother with it? Jesus is wiser than anyone I have ever known."

"Look, here they come," Mary Magdalene pointed to the disciples who were leading the animals to Jesus.

Mary watched Jesus step near the nervous colt and slowly stroke its mane. She could hear Jesus whispering to the animal and making calming noises. She smiled at his gentleness and how he genuinely seemed to care for every living thing.

The two women watched the men take off their outer coats and placed them over the back of the colt as its mother stood by watching all the events. Once they had arranged the garments, Jesus climbed on its back and pointed the animal toward Jerusalem.

As the men followed after Jesus, the two women carefully followed after the group to make their way to the large city. Though Mary considered that Jesus knew full well they were following them and there was no need to do so in secret.

The group of Jesus' disciples began to sing songs as they entered into the gates of Jerusalem.

When the people saw Jesus riding upon the colt, some came running over to him and tried to touch him. Many threw their coats on the path in front of them and when Mary Magdalene saw the excitement of the crowded streets, she came out from the shadows and began to shout her story along with the others. "He cleared my soul of demons!"

Mary followed after her, shouting, "Blessed be the King that comes in the name of the Lord."

The women went to a nearby palm tree and picked up some fallen branches. They placed them on the ground to line the way as Jesus rode in the street of Jerusalem heading toward the Temple. They were running and leaping around in the crowd when they noticed a group of Pharisees coming toward Jesus with a set look of anger on their faces.

They pressed as close as the crowd would allow and yelled at Jesus, "Master, rebuke your disciples. This foolishness needs to cease."

Jesus looked out over the crowd of cheering people. "I tell you that if they should hold their peace, the stones would immediately cry out."

The crowd cheered even louder as Jesus silenced the Pharisees.

"Hosanna!"

"Blessed is he that comes in the name of the Lord."

"Blessed be the kingdom of our father David, which comes in the name of the Lord."

"Hosanna in the highest."

Later, Mary and Mary Magdalene led two young lambs back to Bethany.

"Wasn't that exciting?" Mary Magdalene asked.

"Yes, it was."

"I don't know what came over me. I had so much joy in my soul that I had to let it out."

"I know what you mean."

When they reached the house, the women put the two lambs in the small pen at the back of the courtyard. It had fresh straw that smelled sweet. Mary watched the two young lambs settle in after the long walk before she went into the kitchen to help the others with the food preparation.

It was nearly nightfall before Mary heard the sounds of the group coming into the courtyard. She stepped out of the kitchen and saw the group of men eagerly striding around her house.

"Did you see that?" Simon said.

"I can't believe we escaped with our heads intact," James said.

"That's what I've been talking about," Simon said. "I knew Jesus was holding back on us."

"We shall have the victory over Rome for sure," Peter agreed.

"And we shall sit on thrones as kings!" John yelled.

"What is all this?" Mary asked, searching the group for Jesus.

When he finally entered, Mary's heart fell. His cheeks were flushed and his brow was covered with sweat. She rushed to him with a clean cloth. Wiping his forehead, she asked, "What happened?"

"I-I-I need some fresh air."

Mary held his elbow. "Come, let's walk." She led him to her vineyard and opened the gate. "Tell me what has got those men so excited?"

Jesus took several deep breaths and paced around the vineyard before speaking. "I didn't come for this. I came for something much greater. Mary, if you had seen them today." He turned to face her. "Passover is meant to show mercy and grace. It was never meant to be a profit for those struggling to provide on even the most common of days. It is a chance for all to come to the table as equals in the sight of God. All under His protection. Those sellers were charging so many fees just for a profit."

He turned away and began to walk around again. "The people paying from what they don't have just to obey the law. A relationship with God was never meant to be purchased. It was provided. The cost was transferred to the innocent. These men want power. They don't see that in order to have power, one must be willing to submit. In order to have order, there must first be destruction. They want the easy path of removing Rome and setting up their own system, but that plan will never work. God already has a plan in place and it's nothing like what they think. But it's everything they've been taught. For salvation and continued relationship, innocent blood must be sacrificed." His body heaved with uneven breaths.

"What are you saying?"

"What I've been saying all along." He wiped his forehead with the back of his hand. "My time is drawing near. It won't be long now."

The following morning, Mary and the other women followed Jesus and his disciples to the Temple.

"What do you think will happen today?" Mary Magdalene asked Mary as they walked behind the group.

"I don't know."

"Did you hear the men talking last night?"

"Yes."

"They were talking about a revolt."

Mary looked at the back of the heads in front of her. "I know."

Jesus found a spot in the open porch to teach.

Mary kept an eye out for anyone who would come against him. She wouldn't be able to stand in the gap to fight, but she might be able to signal him if trouble was heading his way.

"Sir," a man called as he approached Philip. "We want to see Jesus. His fame has traveled to Greece. We have traveled here to see him."

Philip called Andrew over. The two talked to Jesus while pointing at the small band of men.

Jesus waved the Greeks over and welcomed

them to sit in the group. He continued his lesson, "The hour is come that the Son of man should be glorified. I tell you the truth, unless a kernel of wheat falls to the ground and die it lives alone, but, if it dies, it brings forth much life. He that loves his life shall lose it. He that hates his life in the world shall keep it forever. If any man serves me, let him follow me, and where I am, there shall my servant be. If any man serves me, my Father will honor him. Now my soul is troubled. What shall I say? Shall I ask my Father to save me from this hour?" Jesus looked up at Mary. "No, for this cause I have come. Father, glorify Your name."

"I have both glorified it and will glorify it again," a voiced roared from the sky.

"Was that thunder?" one of the Greek men asked.

"I think it was an angel," someone in the crowd replied.

Jesus said, "The voice came not for me, but for your sakes. Now is the judgment of the world. Now shall the prince of this world be cast out. If I be lifted up from the earth, I will draw all men unto me."

"Our law says Messiah will live forever," a man in the crowd said. "Why do you say 'The Son of man must be lifted up?' Who is the Son of man?"

Jesus answered, "The light will be with you only for a little while longer. Walk while you have the light, lest the darkness overtake you. For he that walks in darkness doesn't know where he goes. While you have the light, believe in the light, that you may be the children of light."

Mary saw a group of Pharisees heading their way and waved to Jesus. He dismissed the crowd and led his followers back to Bethany for the night.

"It's getting heated," Mary overheard James tell Simon.

"I know," Simon answered. "Jesus says it won't be long now."

Mary stroked the lamb on her lap. She was feeding them in the pen when the men gathered on the other side of the gate to whisper in secret.

They moved away as Jesus came near.

"Mary, may I join you?"

"Yes. I was just tending to the lambs."

Jesus sat across from her and welcomed the other lamb into his lap.

The young animal curled up and fell asleep.

"You have a way with animals."

He smiled.

"And people."

"Some people."

"Most," she corrected.

"I remember when you wouldn't give me more than a few moments of your time. As I recall, you would hardly look at me, much less listen to anything I had to say."

Mary blushed and dipped her head. "I hated you for such a long time."

"Hate builds walls."

"I discovered that all too late."

"And now?"

"Now, I have learned to forgive. Thanks to you."

"Me?"

"Yes. The way you forgave that woman who was captured in adultery." Mary petted the tuft of hair on the lamb's head. "I saw the peace in her eyes after you forgave her. I wanted that peace."

"And have you found it?"

"More than I've had in a long time." She looked up at him. "Thanks to you."

At The Dinner

*"Then took Mary a pound of ointment of
spikenard, very costly, and anointed the feet of
Jesus, and wiped his feet with her hair: and the
house was filled with the odour of the ointment."*
-JOHN 12:3

Wednesday

Mary and Martha were serving Jesus and the
disciples the following morning when a voice
came at the entrance.

"Greetings."

Martha hurried to see who it was. "Please,
come in."

Mary saw Judas Iscariot and his father, Simon,
enter.

"I'll get some water," Martha said, waving the
men into the open courtyard where Jesus sat with
his disciples.

Mary knew it was wrong to stare Judas Iscariot
down, but she wanted him to know she was no
longer intimidated by his presence.

"My father's house is nearby and he has invited

you to a meal," Judas Iscariot said, with a sharp bow to Jesus.

"May I have the great honor of entertaining you?" Simon asked.

Jesus looked between the two men and nodded. "Yes. We shall feast at your house tonight."

Mary glanced over at Martha whose face relaxed into noticeable relief. She got the impression that Martha's bones, which grew tired and more bent over every day, seemed to need a break from serving the multitudes, even if it was for just one meal.

Later in the evening, while the men made their way to Simon's house, the women made their way to the upper room to enjoy a simple meal.

Mary stood in the street as she watched Jesus lead the men toward Simon's house. When the dust settled, she went back into her home.

She found herself staring at the same spot on the floor where Jesus had taught. She knew Martha would handle serving the handful of women without help. Mary's mind went over all the things she had seen Jesus do in her life. Every time, whether he had been in her home or on the streets of the cities, he had shown her nothing but acceptance and care. He had shown great love for her brother and he had shown love for her sister. Jesus had done so many wonderful things without ever asking for a single thing in return.

"Mary?" Martha's voice interrupted her

thoughts.

Mary turned to see her sister rubbing her hands on a cloth.

"Isn't it wonderful? Jesus gave us back our brother and now they can feast together?"

"It is wonderful."

"Then why do you still look so grief stricken?"

Mary turned the ideas over again in her mind. "I'm not sure. Something is bothering my soul."

"Is there anything I can help you with?"

"No, thank you. I believe there is something I must do on my own."

Martha turned back to the kitchen to grab another tray of food.

Picking up her thoughts of Jesus, Mary determined that this single man had done more for her than all of her family or friends combined, yet she had done nothing to show her devotion to him.

Then a thought hit her like a mighty wind knocking the breath out of her.

It was only a few days before the Passover feast. Jesus had repeatedly spoken of his impending death. Maybe he knew that the tide of popularity was turning against him and there were those in leadership that would seek his life. The thought shook Mary to her inward parts and a plan began to form in her mind.

She went to the stairs that lead to the storage room. Making her way down the last stone step and into the open room, she fingered the rows of shelves that her father had built to hold every spice one could possibly imagine. He had made his wealth in trading and selling spices for everything from medicine to burial. The unique, pre-made mixtures were what Mary's eyes were searching for at that moment. Not only did her father have an excellent business sense in always coming out on top of a deal, but he knew how to pamper the people who would spare no expense for their own burial and for any family member who would pass on before them.

Looking deep in the back of the room, she found the small shelf containing the most expensive ones would be able to find in her town or any. She stood staring at the beautiful vessels. Most were made of marble, a few were of white ivory from far away, and a few others were a spiral pattern of a material her father had treasured.

She closed her eyes.

"This one, Daddy," Mary's young voice called from her own memory.

"That, my dear one, is very special." She remembered how her father's eyes danced and a smile lit up his face at the sight of the vessel.

Mary fought back tears as she walked through the recollection.

In her memory, she watched her father carefully reach for the jar and bring it down to her level.

"It's called Alabaster," he said, as he rubbed the bottle between his palms.

Her eyes widened. "It's so pretty."

Her father's smile grew as he allowed her to run her small fingers over the smooth surface.

"And inside," he said, rubbing the sealed top. "Is Spikenard. One of the rarest oils I can get my hands on. Though many have smelled it in its diluted form, only few on earth will have their nose filled with the aroma in its absolute purest form. Its diluted form is traditionally used to help people relax, but because of the strength of its scent it is often used when preparing a wealthy body for burial because it cleanly overpowers the smell of rotting flesh."

"Can I smell it?"

Mary watched her father's face darken.

"I'm afraid not."

Her bottom lip jutted out.

"Now, now, dear one. Look," he said as he turned the small jar in his hand. "It's sealed here at the top. I can't open it just so you can smell it. The alabaster is meant to be broken here at the neck of the jar and the Spikenard to be poured out as a sacrifice. A great one at that."

Her father looked down into her face and she watched his shoulders soften. "But, if you close your eyes and smell right here," he instructed, pointing to the seal. "You can catch the faint scent of it." He held it down to her.

She closed her eyes and inhaled. The fragrance filled her nose and a calming peace washed over her.

"It smells like Mother."

"Yes. It's one of her favorites."

She watched her father place the jar back on the shelf.

"Come on," her father said, as he held out his hand to her. "Let's see if we can find a treat in the kitchen."

Mary smiled at the bittersweet memory as she opened her eyes to see the jars. She carefully picked up the vessel she had come for and held it close to her chest. This one small bottle was worth more than a man could make in a year. The tears begged to be released as she thought about her father and mother and the many happy days they had spent together.

Pulling the bottle away from her chest slightly, she looked down and rubbed the top with her middle finger. The cold wax held back the oil from flowing forth and she knew it held back an even stronger scent.

Rushing back up the steps, she knew this would be it. This would be what she needed to show her devotion to Jesus. She picked up the hem of her dress and made her way down the street toward Simon's house.

The building was not hard to find due to the lavish lifestyle of its owner. Simon was a Pharisee and one of the most elite among them. While men like Mary's father made their riches on long days of hard work, men like Simon had earned their wealth on guilting men like her father into turning over their riches to the priests in order to appease God.

Standing at the main entrance, Mary could hear the male voices flowing from inside the house and bouncing off the large open areas. She took a deep breath, placed the precious vessel in the fold of her dress, and carefully adjusted her headpiece which had come undone in her haste. She was not sure how she would make it past any guards or servants, but neither did she care. She knew Jesus was not far away and nothing would stop her from reaching him.

When she felt the beat of her heart steady enough, she headed toward the voices.

She was staring at the sweet face of Jesus before she realized that no one had seen her, much less had tried to stop her from entering the feast.

The room went silent.

Mary did not have to look around to know that every face would be staring at her in horrific shock, and would not only be male, but also would all be the most prominent men in the area. Simon would entertain no less.

With silence weighing down on her body and the piercing gaze of every man present demanding Mary to turn and flee, one gaze beckoned her to step forward. So, she did. She put one foot in front of the other and made her way to Jesus. He held a slight look of amusement on his face while she slowly drew closer. It was as if he could not only hear her thoughts, but the cursing words of every other person in the room. She had been around him long enough to know he was capable of both.

Jesus lay reclined at a large table, propping his left elbow up on a lavish pillow which allowed his right hand the freedom to bring the exquisite food to his mouth.

Mary slid down to the ground beside his feet and took a deep breath.

Tears came as she looked upon his soiled feet. The stench of the many walks through the dirty streets of Bethany hit her nose. The men who claimed to be so powerful and proper had not even given their most honored guest a foot bath before partaking in this meal.

She gently removed both of his sandals and placed them by her side. Taking his left foot in her hand, she bent down and allowed the tears that were pouring from her eyes to drop onto his dirty foot and then she lifted his right foot and cried on it as well. With both feet soaked with her tears, she noticed she had no cloth with which to dry them. She was certainly not going to ask the men for one since they did not even have the presence of mind to wash Jesus' feet at all. Reaching up with one hand while she held Jesus foot in the other, she pulled her scarf slowly off her head, which allowed her long, black hair to fall freely around her shoulders. She held the cloth in her hand and reached for his foot, but then hesitated.

Snorts of outrage came from different directions as she was sure the men were mentally labeling her a horrid sinner for such actions. Mary knew when she passed through the entrance that whatever status she had left would rapidly decline with each action. Not only had she entered a male only feast uninvited, but also having cleansed the feet of a guest would be a slap in the face of the host whose responsibility it was to make sure all of his guests, and most importantly his honored guest, were cleansed before the meal. And, to add insult to injury, she had removed her headpiece in front of men who were not only not her husband, but also did so openly. She hadn't taken the steps of being declared clean by the priests, but she had chosen to turn her night walking into days of hard labor in her vineyard.

None of that mattered to her as Mary laid the material aside and chose to use her most valued possession instead. Leaning closer, she began to wipe her tears away with her own hair to clean all the filth off Jesus' feet. Though it would have been easier to wipe away the muddy mess with the cloth, using her hair was the last bit of personal honor she could give to this man who had given so much to her and her family.

When she had cleaned as much as she could, she remembered the last thing she wanted to do before this mob of men would seize her and stone her to death for what they had seen done before them. Retrieving the Alabaster vessel from her pocket, she held on to it with both of her trembling hands so she would not spill its contents in waste. Lifting her hands slowly to the edge of the table, she smacked the top of the vessel hard on the corner to break the neck of the bottle. Though it would have been just as easy for her to break the seal at the top, she knew if she broke the neck, it would allow every drop to escape its chamber.

Gasps echoed off the marble walls as Mary heard men shifting all over the place. She didn't care about them; she only cared about the one who was smiling down on her as she carefully moved the bottle over to his body. The strong scent of spicy musk filled her nose as she was almost knocked over by the fragrance.

"Mary!" Lazarus exclaimed at a table across from where she knelt.

She didn't respond and was only urged forward by the growing peace that filled her inside.

Lifting the vessel up, she poured some of the oil onto Jesus' hair and let the pale gold liquid slowly run down his neck. Then she poured the rest onto his feet. Making sure every last drop was poured out onto Jesus, she raised her hands and began to massage the oil into his hair and scalp. She watched Jesus' eyes close slightly as the relaxation took over his body. She noticed his breaths grow deeper and slower as she gently worked the sweet oil into his neck muscles. When she had rubbed all the oil into his hair and neck, she moved to his feet. Messaging the Spikenard into his freshly cleaned feet, she rubbed away the tension and ache she knew would be there from all the walking as he traveled from city to city preaching to the masses.

Once she had finished, she carefully placed each of his sandals back on his feet and tied the straps. As an overwhelming sense of gratitude and love rose inside her, she bent over and began to kiss and stroke the feet she had just anointed. She rubbed her cheeks on his ankles and became overwhelmed with all the memories attached to the scent.

That was the last thing the men could stomach.

"If Jesus was really a prophet," Simon huffed to himself. "He would have known what kind of woman is touching him. She is a sinner."

Mary felt Jesus shift slightly to look over at his host before answering, "Simon, I have something to say to you."

"Master, you are welcomed to speak freely," he groveled.

Jesus took a breath and said, "There was a certain lender who had two men who both owed him debts. One owed him five hundred denarii and the other fifty denarii. When the time came for them to pay their debts, neither had money to pay off their debts. The lender forgave them both. Tell me, Simon, which one of them would love him more?"

Simon paused and thought on the tale before he answered, "I suppose that the man who had the most forgiven, he would love him the most."

"You have judged correctly."

Mary looked up to see Jesus looking toward her, though their gaze was locked, he continued to address Simon. "See this woman?" He nodded gently down at her. "When I entered your house, you gave me no water for my feet, but Mary has washed my feet with her tears and wiped them with the hairs of her head. You gave me no kiss, but she has not ceased to kiss my feet. You did not anoint my head with oil, but she has anointed my feet with a very costly ointment." He turned to the group of men and Mary saw his eyes narrow. "So, I say unto all of you sitting here today, her many sins are forgiven. She has loved much, but the one who has little forgiven, that one loves little." Jesus glanced down to Mary. She watched a warm, gentle smile fill his face. He cupped her chin in his hand and brushed her cheek with his thumb.

"Why has she wasted this?" Judas Iscariot blurted out.

Jesus let go of Mary's face and adjusted himself to face Judas.

"Why wasn't this ointment sold," Judas Iscariot continued, without waiting for an answer. "And the money given to the poor?"

Mary watched Jesus' face turn red before he answered, "Leave her alone. She has done this for my burial." He waved down to her. "You will always have the poor with you, but you will not always have me. She has done what she could. She has come, ahead of time, to anoint my body for burial." With a moist look in his eyes, Jesus turned his attention back down to Mary and cupped her chin again. He raised her glance to meet his eyes. "I tell you the truth," he said while caressing her cheek. "Wherever this gospel will be preached throughout the whole world, what she has done here today will be told in memorial of her."

She smiled up at him. The new familiar peace and warmth flooded her.

He caressed her face one last time before dropping his hand. "Your sins are forgiven," he said.

The men whispered to each other.

"Who can forgive sins apart from God?" one of them asked.

"Only God," another answered.

More whispers flew across the tables as their rage grew hot toward her.

Mary watched Jesus as he noticed Judas Iscariot rise in the midst of the debating men and leave the feast. He took a deep breath and glanced down at her. Forcing a simple smile, he bent close to her ear and said, "Your faith has saved you. Go in peace." He nodded toward the door before he popped a grape into his mouth.

She rose cautiously and slowly backed away, wondering if the still arguing men would follow her out to try to take her life for what she had done. Finding Jesus' gaze, he nodded toward the front again and went back to eating.

When Mary felt the dusty road under her sandaled feet, she turned and ran home.

The tears came as she thought about what had taken place. She had gone in to show her love and devotion for a man who was little more than a family friend. He ended up showing her even more grace and mercy than he had already poured into the empty cup of her life. His love had made the cup overflow. On top of the excess, he added the forgiveness of her sins.

How is he able to do such a thing?

She had given her all to show thanks to him, yet he turned around and freely gave her even more.

Only this could be the Son of God.

At The Passover

"Now before the feast of the passover, when Jesus knew that his hour was come that he should depart out of this world unto the Father..."
-JOHN 13:1

Thursday

"I'm glad we went into the city before the heat of the day," Mary said.

"Yes. Even though the crowds seem to be larger first thing in the morning," Mary Magdalene agreed. "Do you think we have everything for the feast?"

Mary patted the bag that hung over her shoulder. "I hope so."

"Is that Jesus and his disciples?" Mary Magdalene pointed to a group of men sitting near the Mount of Olives.

"I believe it is."

They passed the group of men and overheard their conversation.

"Master," Peter asked. "How are we going to prepare for the upcoming Passover?"

"John," Jesus called. "Go with Peter into the city. There you will meet a man who is carrying a pitcher of water. Follow him to his house. Find the owner of the house and tell him, 'The Master requests the use of your upper room where we are to eat the Passover.' He will show you the room. Make the preparations there and then we will come and join you before nightfall."

The two women shared a glance as they continued to Mary's home.

"Martha," Mary called into the open courtyard. "We have returned."

Martha came out from the kitchen and took the food. "You missed the men. They've been gone for most of the morning."

"We actually saw them on the way back," Mary Magdalene said.

"Yes," Mary said. "They were speaking of Passover plans."

"And?" Martha asked.

"Well, it was the strangest thing," Mary began. "Jesus told Peter and John to go into Jerusalem and look for a man carrying a pitcher of water."

"A man carrying a pitcher of water?" Martha repeated.

"That's what he said," Mary Magdalene offered.

"A man?" Martha sneered. "Must be no women in the house. Fetching water is woman's work."

Mary Magdalene nodded. "I thought we would

be having Passover with your family."

"With Jesus, you never know," Mary said.

"Speaking of which, would you be a lamb and fetch some water for tonight," Martha asked Mary Magdalene. She pointed to the large water pitcher in the corner.

"My pleasure."

"Mary, you can come help me," Martha said. "Even if the men are not going to join us, we still need to prepare for the rest of us."

Mary worked with her sister for the next several hours to prepare a large feast. As the women began to gather in the upper room of Mary's house, she stood in the courtyard watching the doorway. The sun was low in the sky and it would soon be hidden away for the night. She glanced up the ladder as Martha's form disappeared into the room. The voices from the large room encouraged Mary's heart, but there was one voice she desperately wanted to hear. She looked back at the doorway and rushed out.

She ran toward Jerusalem trying to outrun the setting sun and find a single home in the midst of a massive city.

As she turned a corner, she caught sight of James and John entering a house. Rushing after them, Mary found herself in a stranger's courtyard.

"Mary?" a female voice called.

She turned to see a familiar face. "Greetings, Mother." Mary beamed at Jesus' mother.

"Greetings, child." She grinned back. "What can I do for you?" Mary of Nazareth wiped her hands on a rag.

"Nothing." She rushed over to hug her. "I am here to help you."

A look of confusion crossed Mary of Nazareth's eyes. "Why, my dear, aren't you celebrating with your family and the other women tonight?"

"I heard rumors that Jesus would be having the meal here with his men and there were no women to help," Mary said as she picked up some herbs from the table and began to bundle them together.

"You're sweet." She waved around the small kitchen. "When I heard there were no women here, I offered to help too. Though there was not much left to be done. I don't know how the men of this house to do all with no women around. I was putting the final touches on the platters."

Mary heard heavy footsteps above them.

"The last of the group must be here," Mary of Nazareth said. "Come, you can help me bring the platters up to them before they get started."

Picking up a tray filled with chunks of roasted lamb, Mary followed her up the steps to the upper room.

Once they reached the top step, she heard the men talking amongst themselves as she followed Mary of Nazareth's lead in placing everything on the table.

"Thank you, Mother," Jesus said, as he kissed

her cheek.

"You're very welcome."

Jesus nodded to Mary.

She bowed her head, resisting the urge to leap into his arms. She had done enough in front of his men to have her labeled a madwoman. Though her heart ached to be as near as possible to him, she had to restrain herself for honor's sake.

The two women finished setting the table and left the men to their meal.

Mary's mind wandered upstairs as she tried to help clean up the kitchen. Her eyes kept drifting up to the ceiling. When she glanced down, she met eyes with Mary of Nazareth. She blushed and buried her head.

It wasn't long before her curiosity got the better of her and her focus returned to the voices coming from above.

Mary of Nazareth cleared her throat.

Mary looked back down at the bowl she was washing.

"You seem to be distracted," the older woman said.

"I'm just wondering what Jesus is teaching on tonight."

"Well," Jesus' mother said, "I can take care of the rest of the things down here."

"Do you think they would mind if I…" Mary whispered.

The older woman smiled slightly and nodded as she rolled her eyes up toward the ceiling.

"Thank you, Mother." Sneaking on her tiptoes, Mary quietly made her way up the stairs where she could hear the men. A sheer curtain hung in the doorway that hid her from view, so she sat close enough to catch every word.

Peering through the veil, she saw the men reclined around the table as Jesus took the lead. They laughed and joked before the meal began, but settled into quiet respect while she watched as they went through the steps of the Passover.

Jesus poured the first cup of wine and blessed it saying, "And there was evening and there was morning, the sixth day. The heavens and the earth were finished, the whole host of them. And on the seventh day, God completed His work that He had done and He rested on the seventh day from all His work that He had done. And God blessed the seventh day, and sanctified it because in it He had rested from all His work. Blessed are You, Lord, our God, sovereign of the universe, who creates the fruit of the vine."

"Amen," the men answered in unison.

"Who made all things exist through His word."

"Amen."

Mary waited to hear the next part of the Passover start, but there came a long pause.

She peered through the veil as hard as she could and could not believe her own eyes. Jesus rose from his place at the head of the table and took off his outer garments. She watched him pour water into a nearby basin and then he took the towel that was lying next to it along with the bowl and got down on his knees in front of John.

All the men's eyes grew wide as they watched in disbelief. No one had any words as they all watched Jesus wash each and every one of his disciples' feet.

Lastly, he came to Simon Peter. "Lord, why do you wash my feet?" Peter found the words the other men were thinking.

Jesus answered, "What I do now you don't know, but you will understand later."

"You will not wash my feet," Peter said and pulled his feet up under himself.

"If I don't wash your feet," Jesus answered. "You will have no part with me."

"Then, Lord, not only my feet, but also wash my hands and my head." He lowered himself to Jesus.

"He that is washed needs to only wash his feet, but is clean in every way and you are clean." Jesus looked around the room. "But not all of you are clean."

After he had washed their feet, he picked up his outer garments and put them back on before he sat down again. Then he said, "Do you know why I have done this? You call me Master and Lord, and you are right because I am. If I, being your Lord and Master, have washed your feet, you also ought to wash one another's feet. For I have given you an example, which you should do as I have done to you." Jesus looked into each man's face before continuing, "I tell you the truth, 'The servant is not greater than his lord. Neither he that is sent greater than he that sent him.' If you know these things, happy are you if you do them. I'm not speaking to all of you. I know whom I have chosen that the scripture may be fulfilled, 'He that eats bread with me hath lifted up his heel against me.' Now, I have told you this before it comes, so that when it comes to pass, you may believe that I am he."

Mary watched Jesus' face grow dark and then he said, "I tell you the truth, one of you will betray me."

The disciples exchanged glances for several moments.

Mary's heart began to race.

Peter leaned over and whispered to John, who was resting on Jesus, "Ask him who he means."

John turned to Jesus and asked, "Lord, who is it?"

"He," Jesus answered. "That I will give the bread too after I dip it into the oil."

Mary pressed her face against the curtain and watched Jesus take a piece of bread and dip it in the herbed olive oil before giving it to Judas Iscariot.

"What you are going to do," Jesus said, with a voice just above a whisper. "Do it quickly."

Judas Iscariot took the bread, ate it, and looked around the room before getting up to leave. In his haste, he tripped over Mary who was sitting on the top step.

She looked up with fear that he was going to tell the other men she had witnessed their private meal.

He looked down at her with clear disgust on his face. He shook his head and opened his mouth to say something, but then looked back toward the rustling of men on the other side of the curtain. Giving one more repulsed glance at Mary, he rushed down the steps and out into the darkened streets of Jerusalem.

Mary rushed down after him, but met Mary of Nazareth at the bottom step.

She had been stirred by the noise of Judas Iscariot leaving. "What is going on?" she asked.

Mary shook her head and shrugged. "Jesus said..." she began, but looked back up the stairs.

"What?" Mary of Nazareth asked.

But Mary had already rushed back to her seat on the top step to listen to the rest of Jesus' words.

She reached the curtain just as Jesus was speaking, "Now the Son of Man is glorified, and God is glorified in Him. If God be glorified in Him, God shall also glorify Him in Himself, and will glorify Him. I told you that I would only be with you for a little while. You will seek me, but as I said unto the Jews, 'Where I go, you cannot come.' So now I give you a new commandment. Love one another as I have loved you. By this, all men will know that you are my disciples, if you love one another."

He looked around to each one of them and said, "With great desire, I have wanted to eat this Passover with you before I suffer." Jesus took the next cup, gave thanks, and said, "Take this and divide it among yourselves. I will not drink of the fruit of the vine until the kingdom of God comes."

Then, he took bread and gave thanks saying, "Blessed are You, Lord, our God, King of the Universe who brings forth bread from the earth."

"Amen," the men were able to breathe out the reply.

Jesus broke the bread and said, "This is my body which is given for you. This do in remembrance of me."

The thin wafer was passed down the line.

Mary kept watching as Jesus lifted the last cup. She expected to see him set it aside as tradition called for, but he didn't. Instead of signaling the end of the meal, Jesus held the cup to himself and gazed inside it.

Looking into the confused faces of the men, Mary followed their gazes back toward Jesus.

He raised it high into the air and said, "This cup is the new testament in my blood, which is shed for you. I offer it to you."

Mary's bottom jaw hung open wide as she doubted the words she had heard. She searched the men's faces and a confused look was written all over them. Jesus had just declared himself Messiah and in the same breath had proposed a new covenant with the men around the table.

After the shock wore off, the men began to quarrel among themselves.

"If you are bringing the kingdom here, then I should sit at your right hand," John said.

"No, I should," his brother James declared.

"None of you have the passion I do," Simon shouted. "I should have the honor seat."

"I'm the leader of this group," Peter interjected. "If it be any of us, then it should be me."

Jesus cleared his throat. "The kings of the Gentiles exercise lordship over them and they that exercise authority upon them are called benefactors. But you shall not be so. He that is greatest among you, let him be as the youngest. And he that is chief, let him be as low as the one who serves.

"For which is greater, he that sits at meat, or he that serves? Is it not he that sits at meat? But I am among you as he that serves. You are they which have continued with me in my temptations. And I appoint unto you a kingdom, as my Father has appointed unto me. That you may eat and drink at my table in my kingdom, and sit on thrones judging the twelve tribes of Israel. And where I go, you cannot follow me now, but you will follow me later."

"Lord, why can't I follow you now?" Peter asked. "I will lay down my life for your sake."

"Peter, Satan has desired you so that he can sift

you like wheat." Jesus put his hand on Peter's shoulder. "But I have prayed for you, that your faith would not fail. And when you turn back, strengthen your brothers."

"Lord, I am ready to go with you now. Both into prison and to death."

"I tell you, Peter," Jesus said with a shake of his head. "You will deny me three times today before the rooster crows."

Jesus turned to the rest of the group and said, "Let not your hearts be troubled. You believe in God, believe also in me. In my Father's house, there are many mansions. If it weren't true, I would have told you. I go to prepare a place for you. And, if I go and prepare a place for you, I will come again and receive you unto myself. Where I am, there you may be also. And where I go, you know, and the way you know."

"Lord," Thomas said. "We don't know where you are going. How can we know the way?"

"I am the way, the truth, and the life. No man comes to the Father, but by me. If you have known me, Thomas, you should have known my Father as well. From this night forward, you know Him and have seen Him."

"Lord, show us the Father," Phillip pleaded. "And it will be enough for us."

"Haven't I been with you long enough?" Jesus answered him. "Yet, you don't know me, Philip? He that has seen me has seen the Father. Don't you believe that I am in the Father, and the Father is in me? The words that I speak unto you I speak not of myself, but the Father that dwells in me. Believe me that I am in the Father and the Father is in me. Whatever you ask in my name, I will do, that the Father may be glorified in the Son. If you will ask anything in my name, I will do it. If you love me, keep my commandments."

He met eyes with each of his men. "I will pray to the Father and He will give you another Comforter that he may abide with you forever. He will be the Spirit of truth that the world cannot receive, because it doesn't see him. Neither does it know him. But you know him, because he dwells with you, and will be in you. I will not leave you comfortless. I will come to you. In a little while, the world will not see me anymore. But you see me, because I live, and you will live also. In that day, you will know that I am in my Father, and you are in me, and I in you. He that has my commandments, and keeps them, that is the one who loves me.

Mary saw his gaze shift toward her for a moment before he continued, "He that loves me will be loved of my Father, and I will love him, and will manifest myself to him."

Andrew leaned over and asked Peter, "What is he saying? What does he mean, 'In a little while, you will not see me'? Then he says, 'A little while and you will see me, because I go to the Father.' I don't understand what he is saying."

Jesus answered, "Why do you inquire among

yourselves what I mean? I tell you the truth, that you will weep and lament, but the world shall rejoice. And you shall be sorrowful, but your sorrow shall be turned into joy. A woman when she is in labor has sorrow, because her hour has come. As soon as she delivers her child, she doesn't remember her pain anymore because she has joy that her son has been born into the world. Soon, you will have sorrow, but I will see you again. Your heart will rejoice and no one will be able to take away your joy." He continued, "These things I have told you in stories, but the time is coming when I will speak plainly of the Father."

"Yes," Thomas said. "Please tell us plainly and stop talking in stories. We know you know all things. This is why we believe you come from God."

"Do you now believe?" He paused and watched their faces. "Behold, my hour has come and is now. You will all be scattered and will leave me alone. Yet, I am not alone, because the Father is with me. These things I have spoken to you, that in me you might have peace. In the world, you will have trouble, but be of good cheer because I have overcome the world."

Mary saw the men begin to rise, so she hurried down the steps. She found Mary of Nazareth sitting in a side room off the courtyard. She fell next to her and buried her face into the older woman's lap.

Mary of Nazareth brushed some hair away

from Mary's face and rubbed her back. "Now, now, sweet child. What has gotten you so worked up?"

"Jesus-" Mary wept, but the sound of the men's footsteps entering the room interrupted her.

Mary didn't have to turn around to know Jesus was standing behind her looking at the two of them.

She looked up into his mother's eyes.

Mary of Nazareth patted her head and stood.

"Is everything well?" She asked Jesus.

"Everything is well," Jesus said. He kissed her cheek and put his mother's hand in his. He patted the top of it a few times and then let go.

"If you say it is, my son." She kissed his cheek and walked into the kitchen.

Mary, on the other hand, was not satisfied. She stepped closer to search his face.

Jesus smiled, but Mary could see the sadness in his eyes.

"Go ahead," he said to his disciples, without breaking his stare with Mary. "I'll follow in a moment."

The men left one by one.

"Mary," Jesus said. "It will be well. I promise." He stroked her cheek. "Trust me."

Mary wanted to believe the man who had given her so much, but she could not dismiss the cloud that hung in his usually bright eyes.

"Your sorrow will turn to joy."

She simply stared deep into his eyes, trying to

search her mind for a way to ask the questions that burned in her heart.

Jesus nodded a few times. "Trust me, Mary." He stroked her cheek once more and then headed out to join his men.

Mary watched him walk down the street until she could not see them anymore, then she closed the door and went to Mary of Nazareth. "Something is wrong," she blurted out.

"I know," the older woman said. "I know."

"Where are they going?"

She tried to smile, but sadness and worry were taking over in her eyes as well. "Jesus said earlier that he wanted to go pray with the men after the meal. They are heading to the Mount."

"The Mount of Olives?"

She nodded.

"I think I know where they are going." Mary hugged her deeply. "Don't worry, Mother. I'll keep an eye on them."

"God's will be done," she whispered into Mary's hair.

Mary rushed toward the Mount, but kept her distance from the group of men. If they discovered her, she was sure they would ask Jesus to send her away.

It wasn't long before they reached her garden. The garden which she had granted Jesus full access. She told him if he ever needed it, it was there for him.

Knowing the vineyard better than anyone,

Mary entered behind the men and stayed in the shadows.

Most of the group stayed close to the entrance, while Jesus led Peter, James, and John deeper into the garden.

"My soul is exceeding sorrowful unto death," Jesus said. "Wait here and keep watch."

The three men sat under a large tree and faced the entrance.

Jesus walked a few feet away and fell down on his knees. He lifted his face toward the dark sky.

Mary hid behind a row of vines to watch him.

He spoke in hushed tones as his body heaved. "Father, if it is possible, let this cup pass from me. Nevertheless, not as I will, but as You will."

After some time had passed, he rose and walked over to where the three men sat under the tree.

They had fallen asleep.

Jesus hung his head and used his foot to nudge Peter. "Peter, do you sleep? Couldn't you watch for one hour?"

The man stirred and jumped to his feet, shaking his head.

"Watch and pray; otherwise, you will fall into temptation. The spirit truly is ready, but the flesh is weak." Jesus said and then returned to the place he was before. He fell hard onto his knees. "Father, if this cup cannot pass from me unless I drink it, Your will be done."

After praying some more, Jesus checked on his

disciples again.

The three men snored as they slept.

Jesus didn't say anything this time, but went back to his previous spot.

When he knelt again to pray, Mary saw someone appear beside him. A man in a white robe knelt beside Jesus and whispered in his ear. A bright light encircled the man and he had two great wings that grew out of his back. They were like shields of armor shining in the moonlight. The man rested an arm across Jesus' shoulders as he continued to whisper in his ear.

Jesus' sobs grew louder as he prayed, "Father, Your will be done."

The man vanished just as quickly as he had appeared.

Mary searched the area where Jesus was, but she couldn't find the winged being. When she looked upon Jesus again, he wiped his brow on his sleeve.

A glint of red caught her eye and she moved closer towards him. The sweat he had rubbed off his head was bright red. She stifled a gasp.

When she saw him rise, she searched his person for a wound, but found none. His forehead was still covered in red and it dripped down his face. He looked like a man who had encountered a roaming spirit in the past few hours and had lost a wrestling match against said spirit. She desperately wanted to run to comfort him, but she didn't have any words to say.

He came upon the three men who had fallen asleep again. "Are you still sleeping?"

At Jesus' voice, the men stirred and rose slowly.

"It is enough, the hour is come. The Son of man is betrayed into the hands of sinners."

Just then, Mary turned her head at the sound of dozens of feet marching their direction. The sound was all too familiar to her. Her heart raced and she could scarcely catch her breath. She pushed herself deeper into the shadows to stay out of sight.

The light from several torches lit the faces of a band of Roman soldiers and servants marching toward them. There were so many faces, she couldn't count them all. It was as if every soldier assigned to Jerusalem was filing into the garden. There was one face Mary recognized. Judas Iscariot was leading them straight to Jesus.

He came close to Jesus and kissed both of his cheeks.

"Judas Iscariot?" Jesus asked. "Do you betray the Son of Man with a kiss?"

He looked down at his feet and then backed away.

Jesus looked around at the group of men behind Judas Iscariot and asked, "Whom do you seek?"

"Jesus of Nazareth," the group's leader answered.

"I am he," Jesus answered.

At the sound of his declaration, the ground under their feet began to violently shake causing the soldiers to be driven to their knees.

Mary caught one of the vines to keep herself upright.

Jesus asked again, "Whom do you seek?"

"Jesus of Nazareth," came the shaken reply.

"I have told you that I am he. If you seek only me, then let these go their way."

Peter drew his sword and struck a servant standing nearby.

The man's right ear fell to the ground with a thump as he held on to the side of his head. His screams sent shivers down Mary's back. Blood poured through his fingers and dripped onto the ground under him.

"Put away your sword, Peter!" Jesus exclaimed. "Should I not drink the cup which my Father has given me?" He reached down and picked up the ear which had been cleanly removed with the sharp sword.

Mary's stomach turned.

Jesus pushed the servant's bloody hand away from the side of his head and put his ear back into its place. Holding a hand over the ear for just a moment, Jesus held the gaze of the shocked man. When he let go, the ear was completely healed. Only the drying blood on the ground and on the man's hand were evidence that his ear had indeed been cut off.

Then Jesus turned to the officers and said unto

them, "You come out here in the middle of the night as if to capture a thief. You bring swords and staffs to take me. Daily, I was with you teaching in the temple, but you did not take me then. But the scriptures must be fulfilled as they are written."

The captain of the guard grabbed Jesus by the arm, while two other soldiers bound his hands in rope, and then they led him out of the garden.

Mary watched Peter follow far behind the group while the rest of the men went running in different directions leaving her standing there alone in the dark.

She stood there frozen for a moment, listening to the sound of the mob of footsteps trail off into the dark. They were heading east, toward Jerusalem. She didn't know what was going to happen to Jesus next. But she knew who could find out for her.

At The Palace

"When the morning was come, all the chief priests and elders of the people took counsel against Jesus to put him to death:"
-MATTHEW 27:1

Thursday Night

With beads of sweat on her forehead, Mary raced through the streets of Jerusalem searching for the villa of the person who would never turn her away.

The streets were quiet enough for her to easily follow the trail of the band of soldiers who had taken Jesus away. When they headed toward the Temple, she turned the corner toward Joseph of Arimathea's home.

When she reached the gate, she rattled it. "Guard! Guard!"

The same rough man who had given her entrance before rushed toward the gate. "What is the meaning of all this noise? It is enough to rouse the dead."

"I beg you, please allow me to enter and speak to your master."

"My master is not here."

"What?"

"I say again, the master of the house is not in. He was called away a short time ago."

"To where?"

The guard stuck his arm through the bars and pointed. "The Temple."

Without a word, Mary fled toward the Temple. She made it to the grand stairs when she saw a form she recognized. "Joseph," she called out to a man who turned around trying to find the face of the voice.

Noticing Mary's waving hand, he quietly made his way over to her.

"Mary, what are you doing here? It's not safe in the city tonight. Go home," he said, grabbing her elbow and leading her away from the Temple.

"No!" Mary yelled as she pulled her arm away. "Tell me what they are doing with Jesus."

Joseph sighed deeply. "How much do you know?"

"Not much." Mary shook her head. "I saw him in the garden with his followers and then the soldiers came and took him away. Where are they taking him?"

Joseph put his finger close to his mouth and looked around. "There have been more rumors hovering around tonight than flies on the back of a mule. Right now, they are escorting Jesus before the High Priest. They've called the council together, which is illegal in the middle of the night. It's as if they don't care about their own laws anymore because of their bloodthirst," the tone in his voice rose. "Plump men who have spent decades gorging themselves on the best meat of thousands of sacrifices. It was never meant to be this way. The reserve meat was God's way of providing for them to function in their role of servant. These men walk around as if they are prize rams. They have grown fat in flesh and in soul, thinking they are above anyone else. The blood was supposed to cover our sins, yet they have added countless rules to it and I…"

Mary watched his thoughts trail off in his eyes.

"Forgive me. My tongue hangs too loose tonight." He took a breath and adjusted his tunic. "Nicodemus came to fetch me. We were heading in there now to see what else we could find out."

"Please," Mary put her hands together and pleaded. "You have to keep me informed of what happens."

Joseph closed his eyes and nodded. "Just keep out of trouble. As soon as I know more, I will come and find you."

"Thank you, thank you," Mary called as Joseph ascended the large staircase into the Temple.

For a long time, Mary paced around the courtyard of women wondering what was happening behind the doors she could not enter.

Small streams of light flooded the open streets of Jerusalem. In the distance, Mary heard a cock crow. The warm sunlight did little to comfort her.

It should have been most welcomed after a cold night with no sleep, but it wasn't. The only thing she wanted was to be in the presence of Jesus. She wanted to see the light in his eyes and have him smile one more time at her. She wanted to rub her cheeks into his large, rough palm. She wanted to smell his earthy, woody scent. She wanted to tell him that she...

Joseph's form walking out of the gate caught her attention. She picked up the hem of her dress and ran over to him. "Tell me. What is the news?"

Joseph pulled her by the arm to bring her into one of the side rooms before he spoke. "Shh, keep your voice down. They have found Jesus guilty of blasphemy and have placed him in jail."

"Blasphemy! Never has such a thing crossed his lips."

His eyes widened as he looked around. "I asked you to keep your voice down." He did not continue until Mary tightened her mouth and nodded. "They had to wait until daybreak to confirm the verdict. In their minds, Jesus is condemned already. It's just a matter of carrying out sentencing. He will be held for now, but they are calling Pilate out of bed."

"Pilate?"

He nodded. "The High Priest's so-called 'witnesses' couldn't seem to get their story straight. So, they are requesting Jesus be taken before Pilate to see if he will render a guilty verdict."

"Guilty? Why would they want to find him guilty?" Mary tilted her head, trying to understand his words.

Joseph took another deep breath before he answered. "Mary," he said, looking deep into her eyes. "They are trying to find a reason to have him killed."

Mary gasped and covered her open mouth with her hands. "Kill him? Why would they do that?"

Joseph held her shaking elbows and looked around the growing crowd which filled the open courtyard to see if anyone was watching them. "Mary," he looked back down at her. "They want him dead. The High Priest thinks Jesus is nothing but a troublemaker and they want him done away with for good. They want to put this whole business behind them."

Tears blinded her vision as Mary felt her whole body shake. "W-W-What?"

Joseph's head popped up as he noticed the crowd that seemed to shift all at once.

"What is it?" Mary asked, following his eyes.

"Something is happening." Joseph motioned her toward them. "Go, follow the crowd, but stay out of the way. They must have awakened Pilate and are holding court. Be safe and please stay out of trouble."

Mary turned to see the people moving toward Pilate's court and when she turned back to thank Joseph, he had already gone.

Rushing to find a place where she could hear, she listened as Pilate came forward to address the crowd.

"Your High Priest has brought this man before me with the accusation of blasphemy," Pilate said, standing above the crowd. "Seeing as how he is a Galilean, I will send him to Herod, who is in the city for your Passover. Let him deliver a ruling on this man." He turned and headed back inside his palace.

Mary watched the large crowd of people move toward the other side of the city where Herod was staying. Slowly following the group, she tried to stay out of the way, but made sure she kept up with the people.

When the crowd arrived at Herod's Palace, she stood outside in the large, open courtyard. She had no other choice, because no one could enter Herod's court without being invited. She paced around the yard, waiting patiently for any word on Jesus' fate.

As she fidgeted around on the steps of the area for some time, she bumped into a male form. When she turned around, she saw Joseph's eyes staring over her head. Mary turned to see Jesus being brought out before Pilate again.

Joseph motioned with his head that she should follow him.

She followed his lead down the steps and behind the group of people who moved across the city again like a herd of sheep following after their shepherd.

It wasn't until they were back in front of Pilate's palace that Joseph stopped. He pulled Mary to a side street. The two of them waited until Jesus appeared on the balcony with Pilate.

Mary stretched up on her toes to get a better look at Jesus over the crowd.

"Disgusting show," Joseph's voice dripped with disdain. "Herod wanted Jesus to perform for him. Do miracles and such. I think Jesus knew that and he refused to give in to Herod's infantile demands. I'm sure he saw Jesus as a plaything, a doll that he did not find entertaining enough. So, he sent him back to Pilate."

"What is to be done with him now?"

"My guess is that Pilate will interrogate him again," Joseph said. "Ah, see, yes."

Mary watched a soldier lead Jesus behind a curtain after Pilate.

"I'm going to see if I can gather more information. Stay here and I will come to you again." He hurried through the people and disappeared into the depths of the Palace where Mary could never enter.

She wrung her hands and bit her lip. Her eyes watched the curtain for any movement.

Moments crawled by like hours. Then Jesus came out from behind the curtain.

Pilate motioned with his finger and servants brought Jesus across the open stage.

Her heart skipped a beat when Mary saw the

sadness on his face. His entire form was downcast as if he were carrying an unseen heavy burden on his shoulders.

"It's an absolute outrage," Joseph huffed, as he appeared again beside her. "What they are doing to this man is an outrage. It makes one's blood boil. I joined this council to bring order and justice to our land. And this is how they pass judgment?"

"What is it?" Mary asked.

Joseph pointed up to the balcony.

"Why is he bruised?" Mary yelped.

"The soldiers beat him after he held his tongue to their accusations and questions. The Romans are well-trained soldiers. They are great at breaking a man down to the point his willingness to live is replaced by defeat."

A whimper escaped Mary's lips.

"Pilate will hear about this from me. Of that, you can be sure."

Mary glanced back up in the direction Jesus stood.

"They are mocking him since his charge is blasphemy for claiming to be our king. Romans are great at torture and I'm sure those bruises that are forming on his face were given by the hands of the same guards. They've questioned Jesus, but he won't say anything."

"What do you mean he won't answer?" Mary asked.

"I mean, they kept asking him many questions, but Jesus kept quiet the entire time. He refused to answer any of them."

"What does that mean for him?"

Joseph shook his head. "I'm not sure. Pilate has found him not guilty, but has yet to release him."

Both of their heads popped up at the sound of the crowd's chants.

"Crucify! Crucify!"

"Why do they call for him to be crucified when Pilate judged him not guilty?" Mary asked.

"Not only Pilate, but Herod has as well."

Mary's eyes filled with tears and her mouth was filled with silent questions.

"Herod sent him back with no condemnation."

Mary scrunched her forehead. "If both have found him not guilty, he should be released."

Joseph held still.

"You're worried that will not happen?"

He nodded.

"What is Pilate going to do with him then?" Mary asked the question she knew was plaguing his mind.

"I don't know. The High Priest is out for blood. I don't think he will rest until Jesus' blood is spilled one way or another."

Mary raised her hands to her mouth, trying to hold in a scream of panic.

"I'll go and see if I can find out any more. Stay with the crowd. The High Priest has been prodding his bloodlust. Believe me, you don't want to be caught in the middle of all this." He shook his head. "I fear anyone caught supporting

Jesus tonight will sorely regret it tomorrow." With that warning, he fled.

Pilate stood to address the crowd, "You have brought this man unto me, as one that perverts the people and I, having examined him before you, have found no fault in this man concerning those things of which you accused him. Nor did Herod. He has done nothing worthy of death. I will, therefore, scourge him and then release him."

Mary breathed a deep sigh of relief at the thought of Jesus being released by the end of the day.

She caught a glimpse of robed men flowing through the crowd. Each stopped for only a moment to whisper in someone's ear or into a group. Their robes and headcovers revealed their identity. They were the same group of Pharisees that often tried to trip up Jesus in his teachings.

"We don't want him," a man cried from the crowd.

Pilate's head turned toward the sound. "It's custom that, during this feast of yours, I may grant one release of a prisoner to you."

"We don't want Jesus," a different male voice called out. "Release to us another."

Pilate was quiet for a few moments before he motioned over one of his servants. Whispering in his ear, Pilate made a request and then waited for the servant to return. When he did, he whispered in Pilate's ear before being waved off.

"There is one who is held in chains in the

dungeon in Fort Antonius who is called Barabbas. He awaits certain death charged with several crimes."

"Barabbas!" someone shouted.

The name sent a shiver down Mary's back.

Barabbas was a radical who left a sea of blood behind him in his quest for power.

Why would they have him be released over Jesus?

Pilate stood before the gathering. "Whom shall I release to you this feast, Barabbas or Jesus?"

"Barabbas!" a few men shouted together.

"Release Barabbas." More people yelled from different sides of the street.

"Barabbas! Barabbas! Barabbas!" The chant grew from the lips of the people.

Pilate held his hand up to the crowd. "Will I release unto you the King of the Jews?"

"Barabbas."

"Release to us Barabbas."

Mary couldn't believe her eyes or ears. She stared at the faces of the crowd who begged for a murderer to be released back into their society. They wanted this demon over Jesus who had done nothing but healing and good works.

Pilate looked over to his servant and nodded.

The servant returned with two large soldiers. The guards had chains in their hands which held back Barabbas. He looked as if he had spent much of his life living in the wilderness. His hair was wildly untamed, his clothes were slightly torn, and his olive skin was toasted by the sun. Hatred filled his eyes and he looked as if he wanted to spit at Pilate.

Pilate looked over at the servant. The shaking man took an iron key from his robe and came near the prisoner.

Barabbas grinned at the man and licked his lips.

The servant quickly unlocked the chains and stepped back.

The wild man screamed and rushed down the steps and out into the streets.

No doubt blood would be spilled by the end of the day. Mary thought to herself. *How long will Barabbas hold onto his freedom? How long will his pardon last?*

Looking back over at Jesus, Pilate said, "Scourge him." With a hurried movement, Pilate left the balcony.

The people cheered as Jesus was pulled away.

Mary huddled into a ball against the building. She covered her eyes and wept.

At The Scouring

"Then Pilate therefore took Jesus, and scourged him."
-JOHN 19:1

Friday Morning

"Mary?" a soft voice called.

She looked up to see Mary of Nazareth and Mary Magdalene coming toward her. She wiped her face with her sleeve and stood. "Greetings," she whimpered.

"A messenger brought word to your house," Mary Magdalene said. "Calling for Jesus' mother."

"Joseph," Mary whispered. "He must have been trying to reach you and Lazarus with the news. He would have known you were staying with us."

"He spoke of Jesus being imprisoned," Mary of Nazareth said, with concern shaking her voice.

Mary nodded. "He has been convicted of blasphemy."

"Ungrounded charges," Mary Magdalene said.

"The council has convicted him and sent him

to Pilate, who sent him to Herod, who sent him back again."

"Where is he now?" Mary of Nazareth asked.

"Being held for…" Mary's eyes stung.

Mary Magdalene put her arm around Mary's trembling body.

"Pilate ordered him to be scourged," her voice broke on the last word and she leaned on her friend.

"Many survive scourging," Mary Magdalene attempted to comfort her.

"And many don't," Mary bit back.

"When he does," Mary of Nazareth said. "We will take him home and put this whole ordeal behind us."

"That's just it, Mother," Mary said through sobs. "He will not be a free man today. The council put crucifixion in the minds of the crowd and, in turn, Pilate's. I fear that even if Jesus does have the strength to live through the torment of the cat of nine tails, the High Priest's bloodlust will not be satisfied."

"How did you come by all this information?" Mary of Nazareth asked.

"Joseph of Arimathea. He's on the council. He's been updating me as much as he can."

"And you trust this man?' Mary Magdalene asked.

"With my life. He was a friend of my father and he is one of the most honest men I've ever known."

"So, what happens now?" Mary Magdalene asked.

"The scourging will take place in the courtyard inside the Palace." Mary pointed.

"Then we will go there." Mary Magdalene took Mary of Nazareth's hand and began walking.

Mary followed.

When they reached the gate, a guard stopped them. "The courtyard is full."

"This is the man's mother," Mary Magdalene said, pointing to the older woman beside her. "She wishes to see her son."

The man eyed the three women. "And who are you two?"

"We are…"

"His sisters," Mary interrupted.

"Sisters?" the man in the red cloak said with doubt clear in his inquiry.

"Yes," Mary stated sharply.

He eyed them once more before he stepped aside. "Pass."

The women pushed their way through the crowd in an attempt to get closer to the front.

"Sisters?" Mary Magdalene said with a raised eyebrow.

"Officially, I didn't lie. Jesus calls his male followers brothers, so why not call us sisters?"

"Sisters," Mary Magdalene rolled the word in her mouth. "I like it."

"I think of you and the others like sisters anyway," Mary said.

"As do I."

"Look," Mary of Nazareth whispered.

Mary followed her gaze toward the center of the courtyard where a short pillar stood. It and the stones around it were much darker than the surrounding pillars that held up the roof. She knew it wasn't burned by the sun, but from countless men whose blood poured from deep gashes and ripped muscles.

Her breath quickened and her heart pounded in her chest. She gasped for fresh air as the crowd pressed in around her.

I've got to get out of here.

Mary stepped back and was met with a wall of people. She frantically searched for a clear path out of the courtyard.

The sound of ripping flesh filled her ears. The metallic taste of blood tingled at her tongue. The grief-stricken faces of men and women filled her mind's eye.

I can't take another memory of innocent blood being spilled.

Past and near present tangled in Mary's thoughts. She dug into her scalp, trying to slash the images from her mind. Shutting her eyes as tight as she could, she covered her face.

No. Please. God. Stop this.

The crowds' dull murmurs suddenly shifted into thunders of rage.

Mary knew. She knew if she opened her eyes, she would be met with his. Her heart ached, but she couldn't leave her eyes closed forever. So, she slowly opened them. There he was. Held with chains by a Roman soldier on each side. A third soldier was handed a scroll to the officiant standing by.

She found his eyes. Even in the massive mob, Mary could see him and knew he could see her. She shook her head. She noticed some fresh markings on his face as if he had been struck several times recently. These did not make it past the careful eye of the official either, who looked at the soldiers with deep suspicion before nodding his approval.

Please. No.

She thought she would see grief or even anger in his eyes, but no. She saw…*Love?*

She fought back the tears filling her eyes.

Mary Magdalene turned around in front of her.

Mary shook her head and bit her lips.

Her friend reached back and held out her hand.

Mary took it and stepped forward beside them again. Swallowing the large lump in her throat, Mary looked back at Jesus.

The soldiers disrobed him and brought him toward the short pillar. They fastened his chain to the metal ring and stepped aside.

Mary could barely breathe and she held tightly to Mary Magdalene's hand.

The taller soldier shook out the whip in his

hand to make sure it was prepared. The long strap held pieces of broken iron, clay, and glass, along with jagged stones and any other sharp objects they could find. All of the pieces were tied to the ends of each length of leather.

The clang of glass and metal sent a tremor down Mary's back and made her knees go weak. For a moment, she feared she would pass out. She squeezed Mary Magdalene's hand to ground herself and her friend squeezed right back.

The soldier reached his arm over his head and brought the cat of nine tails straight down onto the side of Jesus' back.

"One," the officiant called.

With every hit, the sharp pieces dug into the soft flesh and then with a twist of the wrist, it ripped flesh and muscle out of place. Blood dripped down his back and legs at first, but by the tenth blow, it poured freely.

Mary let go of Mary Magdalene's hand and stepped closer to the two women. She turned her face away from the blood that began to pool. She saw the face of Mary of Nazareth who was staring with wide eyes at the tragedy unfolding before her. Grief was written all over her aged face.

Mary had never held a child from her womb, much less watched a son be scourged. She reached for the older woman as she wished she could reach for him. She wrapped her arm around Mary of Nazareth's shoulder and pulled her close.

Mary of Nazareth collapsed into her.

Mary could feel the heartbroken mother jump with each hit.

She stood by and watched once again as innocent flesh was ripped open and blood poured out to stain the sand below. There was nothing she could do all those years ago and there was nothing she could do now.

While the counting continued in an agonizing and prolonged manner, Mary focused on the woman under her arm. She loved this woman, the one after whom she was named. This woman and her own mother were the best of friends. Both came from devout Jewish families and had spent much time in Jerusalem together. They had formed a special bond that transcended the miles between their two cities.

Mary remembered their first meeting.

When Joseph had brought Mary from Nazareth to Bethlehem to be counted in the census, Mary remembered how happy her mother, Eila, was at the thought of spending time with her friend. They had not seen each other in years and Mary had sent word that she would be bringing a surprise with them.

Mary and Joseph of Nazareth came to Mary's home in Bethany a few weeks after the census. She remembered seeing her for the first time. Her eyes seemed to light up from the inside out.

She practically beamed when her mother introduced Mary to her friend. "Mary? After me?"

"What else would I call my daughter? You're

my best friend," Eila explained.

Her father and mother had welcomed them graciously into their home with a giant feast. They all ate and laughed the rest of the day. The grownups shared many stories over the meal and Mary enjoyed listening to them all.

The surprise Mary of Nazareth had brought was a tiny bundle wrapped in swaddling clothes. A baby boy named Jesus.

"Jesus? Why Jesus?" Mary asked.

Mary and Joseph shared a smile.

"That, young one," Joseph said, as he raised her into his lap. "Is a very wonderful story."

"Oh, do tell us," Eila said, rubbing her large belly.

Joseph cleared his throat. "Mary and I had been betrothed for some time while I was working on building a proper home for us. She came to me to tell me she was going to have a baby. Well, I knew this could not be my child because I had not taken her to be my wife yet."

"I was so frightened you wouldn't believe me," Mary of Nazareth said.

"I didn't at first," Joseph said. "I was even planning to divorce you privately."

"You're a good man," Johnathan said.

"I loved her." Joseph looked at him. "I didn't want to make a public display of her. People can be so mean as it is."

"What made you change your mind?" Eila asked as she popped another olive into her mouth.

"Well, the night before I was going to talk to Mary, I had a dream. An angel of the Lord came to me and told me that she was telling the truth. That God had made her pregnant and the baby would be a man of God. He gave me clear instructions to take her as my wife and to care for the child as my own. The angel also told me to call the baby Jesus, because he would save us all."

"Him?" Mary pointed to the baby. "But he's so little."

Joseph laughed. "Yes. But even the greatest men of God start out little."

"Would you like to hold him?" Mary of Nazareth asked her.

She looked over to her mother.

"It's alright, dear. She will show you how."

Mary of Nazareth brought her baby over while Mary was still sitting on Joseph's lap. "It's very important to hold his head." She gently placed him in her arms.

Joseph helped support his weight. "You're a natural."

"There now," Mary of Nazareth said with a smile. "Just like that."

"She needs all the practice she can get with a little brother or sister coming," Johnathan said and kissed his wife.

"I'm going to need your help, Mary," Eila said.

"I promise, Mother." She looked down at Jesus' face. He was perfect. His skin was so smooth and his eyes were as bright as his mother's.

"Greetings, Jesus. I'm Mary."

Joseph chuckled. "I think he likes you."

"You're going to make a great big sister," Mary of Nazareth said.

"Thirty-seven." The loud tally from the official brought Mary's attention back to the moment. "Thirty-eight."

Mary looked down at the same woman who was now soaking her dress with tears. Her eyes weren't bright anymore. It was as if all the light had left her.

"Thirty-nine."

Mary saw the officiant raise his hands toward the soldiers. The signal to cease.

Though forty lashes was the sentence, they stopped at thirty-nine, just in case they had miss-counted. The Romans were known for their rules. They were nothing if not rigorous and careful to follow their own laws. A small reprieve for such a severe punishment.

Jesus' body hung by his muscular arms on the short pillar. Flaps of skin on his back moved with his struggled breaths. He could barely stand on his own.

Two guards unchained Jesus and dragged him away.

"It's over now," Mary whispered into Mary of Nazareth's ear. "They are done."

"Do you think they will let us see him now?" she asked through broken sobs.

"I don't know."

"They must release him now," Mary Magdalene said. "They have had their bloodbath. Surely, it is enough."

The women moved with the crowd toward the open area where they could view Pilate.

They waited as Pilate entered and sat on the throne while Jesus was brought before him. The guards had left him exposed and many people cried out with hatred at the display.

Mary felt someone pull on her sleeve. She turned to see a familiar face. "Aunt Mary?"

"Sister," Mary of Nazareth said. "What are you doing here?"

"Word has spread all around about what is happening in Jerusalem. Martha and Lazarus told me that it involved Jesus and I hurried here as fast as I could." She wiped sweat from her brow.

Joanna and Susanna followed behind her.

"Who is that?" Aunt Mary asked, pointing to the balcony.

"My son," Mary of Nazareth cried and leaned against Mary."

"If you had not told me that the heap of flesh now standing before us was he, I would not have known who he was."

Mary looked back toward the bloody and broken body. "They scourged him."

"What is on his head?" Aunt Mary asked.

"It's a crown," Mary answered. "A crown the guards fashioned out of thorny vines."

"Behold, this poor creature standing before

you." Pilate's words interrupted their conversation.

The small group of women, held together by the beaten man standing for his final judgment, turned to see Pilate rise and address the crowd. "What should I do with Jesus that has been called Christ?"

People around them cried out, "Away with him. Away with him. Crucify him."

The royal general rubbed his dark bearded chin and searched the crowd as if looking for a reprieve, but found none. He spoke, "Shall I allow you to crucify your king?"

A call came from the other side of the crowd, "We have no king except Cesar."

A thunderous laugh spread through the crowd along with cheers.

"I don't believe my ears," a man's voice said beside Mary.

She turned to see Joseph of Arimathea. "What more do they want?" she pleaded. "They have already beaten him, condemned him with false witnesses, and torn the flesh from his back. What else do they want?"

Joseph looked solemnly at the angry faces of the crowd and landed on the smiling face of Caiaphas. "They want every drop of blood drained from his veins and the last breath to escape his mouth."

Fear rose inside her as the chant coming from the crowd gained strength.

"Crucify him! Crucify him!"

Pilate looked down on the cheering people and then back at Jesus before nodding to his aide who signaled two soldiers to grab Jesus and lead him away.

"He is going to give in to their demands?" Mary moved out of the way of the shifting group.

"Yes." Joseph searched the sky. "I need to make preparations." Then he blended into the mass exodus of people.

Shaking his head violently, Pilate called to his servant and made a quiet request.

Upon reentering, the servant brought a large bowl to Pilate. The governor dipped his hands into the bowl and rubbed them together.

Lifting his dripping hands high into the air, he called out, "I am innocent of the just blood of this person. If you want him crucified, then you do it yourselves."

"His blood be on us and our children," a man screamed up at Pilate.

The servant offered Pilate a clean linen.

Pilate snatched it and rubbed his hands on it while he walked back into his palace.

"Crucify! Crucify!" The High Priest rallied the crowd into a chant as the guards pulled Jesus away.

The women followed the crowd as Jesus was led through the city on his way to be crucified.

At The Third Hour

"And it was the third hour, and they crucified him."
-MARK 15:25

Golgotha, 9 AM

Sunlight was beginning to warm the spring day that should have been one of celebration. Mary's heart ached to go back to the festivals and lighthearted life. She had been able to give up being a harlot and finally felt freedom and love as one of Jesus' followers. All her peace and happiness was now staring death in the face. The death of her teacher. The death of her dearest friend. The death of Messiah.

The path toward the hill was well worn. Mary had never taken part in one of these humiliation walks before. Forcing the criminal to carry his crime label around his neck through the city was just another inhumane tactic of Rome. In addition, the guards made Jesus bear his own crossbeam. His back was torn to shreds from the scourging. It was a wonder to her how he could possibly have the strength to accomplish the feat. The wood rubbing against his open flesh must have been excruciating.

When she was able to catch a quick glimpse of his face in the crowd, it was contorted and discolored. With every step, his agony became clearer. After stumbling under the weight of the wood a few times, the Roman guards became impatient.

"Keep moving," one said with a swift kick to Jesus' side.

"Can't you see, he can't!" Mary shouted, but her words couldn't compete with the crowd.

"I said rise," the armor-clad soldier demanded.

"Well, I'm not carrying it for him," another soldier said, as he leaned on his spear.

"Nor will I," the first replied. He searched the pressing crowd. Grabbing the nearest man, he pulled him up to his toes. "Pick that up," he said, thrusting a fat finger to the beam.

"I don't know this man." The man shuddered under the grip of the guard. "I have nothing to do with him."

"I don't care," the soldier said and tossed him down. "Pick it up and let us get to the hill."

With the weight lifted from his shoulders, Jesus was able to rise and finish the journey out of the city under his own power.

Mary stayed below with the other women and most of the crowd while the guards led the prisoners up the hill. She could see them all gather at the top, as her group settled in a place where they would be able to witness everything.

She could see a soldier; his red cape blew in the wind. His hand held a giant hammer that he repeatedly brought down. Though she could not see it, she knew that hammer would land on a long spike set into the wrist of Jesus. The guard would repeat the process until the spike was driven through flesh and wood and the end of it would come out the other side.

Jesus would be lying down on a large piece of wood with the cross beam under his shoulder blades. A triangular piece of wood would be placed under his feet and another spike driven through his feet to keep them on the foot support.

After making sure Jesus was secure on the cross, the soldiers hoisted it high into the air so that all could see. When the cross found its place in the carefully dug hole, the loud thud sent a shiver down Mary's back.

Two other men were hoisted on their own crosses on either side of Jesus.

The three naked bodies nailed to the wooden crosses made Mary blush and turn away. She had gotten used to seeing the uncovered male form in her previous life, but a short time away from that work had reclaimed the indignity of it all.

Above Jesus' head, they had nailed the sign he had worn around his neck through the city.

"What does it say?" Mary Magdalene asked, pointing to the sign.

"Jesus the Nazarene, King of the Jews," Mary translated out loud. "Normally, if a sign is hung above a condemned man's head, it reads the charge of which he is being punished."

"It sounds more like a statement instead of a charge."

"It does." Mary looked up into the sky and noticed it was about the third hour. The events of the day had taken place so rapidly that she would have thought it much later. Her body ached with sadness and exhaustion. She sat down beside Jesus' mother and the rest of his female followers.

The High Priest walked by and began to mock Jesus, "You, that said you would destroy the Temple and build it in three days, save yourself. Come down from the cross and we will believe you."

Likewise, the chief priests who watched the scene said, "He saved others, but he can't save himself. Let Messiah, the King of Israel, come down from the cross that we might see and believe."

Mary of Nazareth tightened beside Mary as even more passed by and spat their disdain. "Haven't they mocked him enough?"

"Pay them no attention," Mary comforted. "This is their entertainment."

At The Fourth Hour

"Then said Jesus, 'Father, forgive them; for they know not what they do.' And they parted his raiment, and cast lots."
-LUKE 23:34

Golgotha, 10 AM

Mary could barely look up. Every time she did, she met his eyes. Those gentle eyes that looked at every person as if they were the only one in the room. Then she would watch his eyes closed as he used what strength he had to push up to take a breath. Though she couldn't see, Mary knew his raw back was scraping against the wood with his every breath.

She looked down and tried to focus on the face of the women around her.

Mother sat near her. The older woman gave comfort by her mere presence. Mary hoped she was providing the same for her.

Mary Magdalene flanked Jesus' mother as if the two younger women were standing guard against the unimaginable pain with which she must be struggling.

Susanna sat with Joanna behind them. They had become a good pair. Mary envied the group of women. The years and miles they had spent together made them more than friends, it had made them family. Watching them work together in a kitchen was like watching a perfectly timed dance. Each had their role and each took up any rare slack without complaint. Mary had Martha, but Martha was always busy taking care of Lazarus and the house. Even after Lazarus was raised from the dead and had full health, unlike anything he had experienced in his life, Martha still found ways to fill her time that didn't include her sister.

"Father," Jesus' voice caught Mary's attention. "Forgive them. They don't know what they are doing."

"He forgives them?" Mary Magdalene asked his mother. "Even now?"

Without turning her gaze away from the hill, she nodded.

Mary looked back toward the hill and noticed a handful of soldiers gathered near the bottom. They formed part of a circle and she saw them casting lots. In the middle of them lay a set of garments. She glanced up at Jesus' naked body and then back to the men. "They are not."

"Not what?" Mary Magdalene asked, peeking over Jesus' mother's head.

Mary nodded in the direction of the group.

"Casting lots for his clothes."

Mary of Nazareth gasped.

The grins on the soldier's faces made Mary sick to her stomach as they divided up Jesus' only garments among the winners. She wanted to run over and tear the precious pieces of cloth out of their hands, but she didn't. She couldn't. She just sat and watched as the Romans slowly took Jesus away from them piece by piece, away from her, with every passing moment.

"I made that garment for him," Mary of Nazareth's voice interrupted her anger. "When he was first preparing to leave to be a traveling teacher. I was so nervous when he told me. He was such a good craftsman. I knew God was going to use him, but I didn't want to give up my son. I didn't want him to travel so far from home." Mary saw the glint in the woman's eyes. "The day he left, I surprised him with that gift. I told him travelers don't often get the comforts of home. So, if he was ever lonely, to wrap up in that garment and remember me and his siblings and our home."

Mary tightened her grip around the woman's shoulders. She could feel her begin to sob again.

Hours passed as the women sat watching Jesus take breath after agonizing breath. Crucifixion was the cruelest way to die. In most cases, men hung for days before death would finally end their misery. Mary was not sure how long Jesus would hang on his cross due to the fact he had already lost so much blood during the scourging. Plus, with each hour that passed, the coming Passover

Sabbath drew closer. A body hanging on a tree would bring a curse on their land. How long would the High Priest let this continue before they demanded the men removed?

At The Fifth Hour

*"When Jesus therefore saw his mother, and the
disciple standing by, whom he loved,"*
-JOHN 19:26

Golgotha, 11 AM

Three men hung heavy on their crosses. The two
on each side of Jesus were easier for Mary to
watch. Even though they were naked, they had not
endured the savage scourging Jesus had gone
through before being nailed to his cross.

One man pushed himself up and said to Jesus,
"If you are Messiah, save yourself and us."

The other scoffed and rebuked him, "Don't
you fear God? You are under the same
condemnation, but we have been judged fairly.
We are being punished for the crimes we know we
committed." He dropped himself down and
struggled to push himself back up to speak again.
This time, he directed his words toward Jesus.
"This man has done nothing wrong." His body
shook under its own weight and his next words
shook along with it. "Lord, remember me when

you bring your kingdom." He unlocked his knees to give himself a break.

Mary saw a peace cover Jesus' face. He looked at the man who spoke to him and between gasps of breath managed to say, "I tell you the truth, today you will be with me in paradise."

"Only the Son of man can make such a promise," a male voice said behind Mary.

She turned over her shoulder to see John's face. "John!" Stumbling to her feet, she embraced him.

He pulled her back to arm's length.

Mary could see his red, swollen eyes.

"Women." He held his arms out.

The other women stood and hugged him in one large group.

Except for Jesus' mother. She slowly rose to her feet, but stayed where she was.

"Mother," John said, waving her into his arms. "Can you forgive me?"

"There is nothing to forgive." She rushed to embrace him. "You were scared as anyone in their right mind should be."

"I should have stayed here with you," he said into her hair. "It wasn't right to run. I got halfway to Galilee before I turned around. I couldn't leave him." He looked up at Jesus. "He has done so much for me."

"For all of us," Mary Magdalene added.

"I was so worried about all of you." He looked over each face. "If the Romans-"

"Hush that kind of talk," Mary of Nazareth interrupted. "We are safe. They have no reason to touch us."

John looked around. "Have any of the others come back?"

"No," Mary said. "You are the only one."

"But all of you are here together?" John said.

"All we have is each other," Joanna answered.

John looked up to the top of the hill. "How long has he been up there?"

"Since the ninth hour," Mary answered.

"Why does he look so awful?" John asked.

"They scourged him first," Mary whispered. The bloody images clawed at the corners of her mind.

"As if this is not enough torment?" John waved his hand up toward the hill.

"Woman," Jesus rasped.

"He speaks?" John said, stepping closer to the hill.

"When he can," Mary said.

"Woman," Jesus said again with another slow lift of his shaking body.

Mary of Nazareth stepped closer.

"Behold your son."

She looked at John.

"Behold, your mother," he said before he collapsed.

"I'll take care of her as my own," John shouted up to Jesus. "That I can promise you. I will never forsake her." He wrapped his arm around Mary of

Nazareth's shoulders and pulled her in close to himself.

She laid her head on his chest and wept.

At The Sixth Hour

"Now from the sixth hour there was darkness over all the land unto the ninth hour."
-MATTHEW 27:45

Golgotha, 12 PM

As the sun came to the highest place in the sky, Mary wiped away the sweat from her brow. The small amount of shade the hill provided had grown small in the midday. Her group edged closer to the hill in order to take advantage of what shade they could.

"How much longer is this going to go on?" John asked.

"It could take days," Mary said. "Though, with everything Jesus has endured, I'm sure his suffering is almost over."

Out of nowhere, the brightness around them from the sun turned to the darkest black Mary had ever experienced. It was darker than any cave or night her eyes had ever seen. A shiver ran down her back as the air quickly cooled around her.

Gasps and screams flew around her. She sat

still feeling carefully around her. When her fingers brushed a garment, she called, "Who's there?"

"It's me, Mary Magdalene," the familiar voice said. "What happened? I can't see anything."

"I don't know," she said. "I thought I had gone blind."

"No, it's all over," Mary said.

"Peace women," John's voice called from the darkness. "Stay still. Give your eyes time to adjust."

Mary stayed perfectly still and waited. It felt like forever, but her eyes finally grew accustomed to the dark. She began to make out the faces of those around her. Each one held a fearful expression like prey cornered by a hunter in the night.

"My God, my God," Jesus cried from the top of the hill. "Why have you forsaken me?"

Mary Magdalene turned to Mary and asked, "Why does he weep so?"

She just shook her head and looked back up at the blackened sky. Her eyes could see some distance now and she looked up into the bloody face of Jesus.

The hidden words came rushing forward in her mind and she began to whisper, "My God, my God, why have You forsaken me? Why are You so far from helping me, and from the words of my roaring? Oh, my God, I cry in the daytime, but You hear me not; and at night, but I find no rest."

"But You are holy," Mary of Nazareth joined her. "Oh, You that inhabit the praises of Israel."

The two women joined together in reciting the old psalm, "Our fathers trusted in You. They trusted, and You did deliver them. They cried unto You and were delivered. They trusted in You and were not confounded. But I am a worm and not a man. A reproach of men and despised of the people. All they that see me laugh me to scorn. They shoot out the lip. They shake the head, saying, 'He trusted on the Lord that He would deliver him. Let Him deliver him, seeing he delighted in Him.'"

The women paused as they glanced toward each other and then looked to the one thief on the hill and to the High Priest. The men had unintentionally mocked Jesus with the words from the poem.

Mary looked at Mary of Nazareth and recited, "But you are he that took me out of the womb. You did make me hope when I was upon my mother's chest. I was cast upon you from the womb. You are my God from my mother's belly."

Mary watched Mary of Nazareth close her eyes as tears rolled down her wet cheeks.

Mary of Nazareth picked up the next line, "Don't be far from me. For trouble is near. For there is none to help." Then she covered her face and wept.

John wrapped her in an embrace.

Mary Magdalene asked, "What is that?"

"A poem of our people," Mary said, in a daze. "A passage we learn as children."

"Is there any more?"

Mary looked at the crowd and said, "Many bulls have surrounded me. Strong bulls of Bashan have beset me round. They gaped upon me with their mouths, as a ravening and a roaring lion. I am poured out like water, and all my bones are out of joint. My heart is like wax, it is melted in the midst of my bowels. My strength is dried up like a broken pot and my tongue cleaves to my jaws. You have brought me into the dust of death. For dogs have circled me. The assembly of the wicked has enclosed me. They pierced my hands and my feet..." Mary paused and glanced back up at the top of the hill.

"They pierced my hands and my feet," she repeated. Mary of Nazareth quieted her weeping and picked up where Mary stopped. "I may tell all my bones. They look and stare upon me."

Mary found the soldiers who had played lots earlier. "They part my garments among them," she said. "And cast lots upon my clothes."

Jesus' mother closed her eyes and raised her head to the murky sky. "But be not far from me, oh Lord. Oh, my strength, hurry to help me. Deliver my soul from the sword and my darling from the power of the dog."

"I think it's about him," Mary said.

"What makes you say that?" Mary Magdalene

asked.

"It all fits."

"How?"

"It's so specific. The people watching would mock, bringing close to death, pierced hands and feet, casting lots for his clothes...So much of it fits, fits right now in this moment."

"He brought it to our memory," John said. "He began the psalm with the first lines."

"That's right," Mary realized. "He said the first lines knowing we would remember the rest."

"Do you think he is trying to tell us something?" John asked.

"Isn't he always?" Mary searched each mourning face that surrounded her. They looked scared and confused. She was beginning to put all the pieces together. Like a broken clay jar in her mind, the cracked parts were starting to fit like they should. Jesus was sacrificing himself. Sacrificing his body, his blood, himself for them. Jesus lived his life showing them how they ought to live and his final and greatest act was this. She was witnessing it with her own two eyes. She saw the man whom she had grown to love more than the flesh that protected her body. He had become her very reason for taking her next breath and yet there he hung, waiting for death to take him and he seemed willing to go.

Just then, Mary thought she caught Jesus' head slightly nod.

She forced her thoughts toward him, knowing

he could hear every one of them. *That's it, is it not? All the pieces fit together perfectly. You told us. You already told us the plan. We just didn't want to hear it.*

Again, his head nodded, just enough for Mary to catch it.

She recalled everything she had heard from his lips and rethought on each one until one stuck out.

His voice rang from her memory, "Let these sayings sink down into your ears for the Son of man will be betrayed and delivered into the hands of men. And they will kill him and the third day after he is killed, he will be raised again."

Mary met Jesus' red eyes. *It's not over, is it?*

Jesus slightly shook his head.

This is not the end, is it?

Another shake.

You have more to teach us?

A brief smile turned into a wince of pain as he struggled for another breath.

Suddenly the winds shifted and a sweet smell crossed Mary's nose. It was strange and yet familiar all at the same time. She closed her eyes and inhaled deeply trying to place the intoxicating scent. With one more deep breath, her eyes flew open in realization. Spikenard. Mary found the gaze of Jesus and could wager he was smiling down at her even through the pain. The sweet scent of her love and devotion was still evident on his skin.

"Mary." Her name came not from his lips, but his voice in her memories.

As they gazed into each other's eyes, Mary knew then what he had been trying to tell, no, show her, what he had been trying to show all of them. All of the lessons came flooding back over her.

Everything makes so much sense. This will not be in vain. His death will not be in vain. He is dying for me; for all of us. This was Jesus' way of pouring out his love and devotion onto them, onto me. The blood that drips down and sprinkles the ground under him is for us. It would be the sweet oil that would mark us as his beloved ones.

The cup, she remembered the cup from the Passover meal he shared with his disciples the night before. He should have set it aside, but instead, he took it and asked his followers to drink from it, asking them to be bound to him.

All the lessons he taught and all the times he told them raced through Mary's mind. He came right out and told them over and over again that this was going to happen. No one listened. No one believed that this would be the way he would bring his kingdom.

Mary believed. Though she still didn't understand all of it, she understood enough. Everything he had said was true. He is Messiah and this was his way of bringing them to God.

At The Edge

> *"Thou lovest righteousness, and hatest wickedness: therefore God, thy God, hath anointed thee with the oil of gladness above thy fellows."*
> -PSALM 45:7

Golgotha, 2 PM

Over the cackling screams of temporary victory that only he could hear, Jesus tried to focus on the faces of those who had followed him for the past few years.

Each breath took him closer to the last he would breathe. He deeply inhaled the overpoweringly sweet scent of the oil Mary poured over his head just a few days before. Each breath filled his nose and lungs with the sweet smell of the perfume, the love she had poured out on him.

Now it was his time to pour his love out on this woman, and this one, and this one as he saw the faces of those gathered around the cross and looked into eternity past and eternity future to see all the faces that would call out for his love. One more time, he breathed deeply that sweet smell of love and released his scent of love on all those who would trust him. They didn't understand. Not yet. But they would.

At The Ninth Hour

"When Jesus therefore had received the vinegar,
he said, 'It is finished': and he bowed his head,
and gave up the ghost."
-JOHN 19:3

Golgotha, 3 PM

Jesus took a deep breath as he pushed himself up on the block of wood. "I thirst!" he yelled.

Mary saw one of the guards pick up a long stick that looked very much like a hyssop stalk and wrapped a piece of cloth on the end. He walked it over to a small bucket sitting beside them and dunked the cloth end into the liquid.

According to Roman custom, the bucket would contain a mix of vinegar and water. The guards were allowed to offer this drink up to those condemned to death on the cross. It would ease the intense thirst and pain that resulted from a slow death of struggling for their every breath.

The armored man lifted the stick high into the air and placed the cloth end near Jesus' mouth so that he could taste the liquid.

Mary watched Jesus slightly open his mouth and suck on the cloth.

When he had a simple taste, he turned his head and the guard placed the stick back on the ground.

"All who are thirsty, come to me," Jesus' words repeated in her memory. She could see his face that day in the temple. His cheeks were red and his eyes shone bright. That festival was the last one at which she had seen all of his siblings. After Jesus' outburst, they had gone back to Nazareth and stayed far away from Jerusalem.

Her own soul had found the quenching reality when she trusted his claim to be Messiah. Though her tongue still dried from the day's heat, her soul had rivers of water rushing through it. Just as he had promised those many months ago.

When Jesus had received the vinegar, he said, "Father, into your hands, I commit my spirit." Struggling with every ounce of his strength, he pushed himself up once more on the block of wood his feet were nailed to and cried even louder, "It. Is. Finished." Then he released the hold on his body and bowed his head.

Mary noticed that his chest no longer moved with breath and his body hung lifeless on the cross. She began to rise and reach out for him as if she could touch him even though she was several feet from him and he was lifted high into the sky.

Just then, the earth under her feet began to shake violently and she heard many cry out in fear. Looking around, she found Mary of Nazareth's eyes as she watched the ground move under her. She went to the older woman and held onto her for the several moments that it took before the land stopped its movement. John had enveloped them both and held on tight. When the shaking ceased, they all clutched each other waiting for the next shock to come.

Jesus' mother pointed Mary's attention to the hill.

Mary saw two soldiers walk over to the crosses, each carried a large staff in their hands.

Another was standing not far off and yelled at the others, "It's nearing sundown, break the legs so that we can get them off theses crosses! We don't want to deal with Pilate if we leave these Jews hanging around on their Sabbath."

The two guards stood under each of the thieves that hung on either side of Jesus and hit the men's legs hard enough that loud cracking sounds echoed from the blows, followed by several shouts of agony. With the men's legs now broken, each was unable to lift themselves up to take a breath and they frantically gasped for air.

After several moments, their bodies became still and lifeless before Mary's eyes.

When the two met in the middle to break Jesus' legs, they found what she had feared; he was already dead.

The taller man turned to the other and said, "We need to make sure he's dead before we can take him down."

The other man nodded and picked up a long spear. He hoisted it high into the air and pierced the side of Jesus' body. When he removed the end of the spear, blood and water flowed out of the wound. He took a step back from the sight and he said, "Truly this man was the Son of God."

Mary felt Mary of Nazareth leave her side. She met eyes with John, who shrugged. They both hurried after the woman who was climbing her way up the path to the top of the hill.

As they reached the top, Mary saw the guards lowering the last cross while the others had begun to pry the other dead bodies off the wood.

She saw Jesus. His eyes were wide and his mouth hung slightly open. She wept for the man who had taught her so much and had given her everything that God had promised to His people.

John caught up to Jesus' mother and held her back.

The three watched the soldier pull the large iron nails out of Jesus' wrists and feet. The wounds were deep, but since the blood had ceased to flow through his body, nothing came out of the holes that now scarred his precious flesh. Even the large slice in his side had stopped flowing with blood and water. The loose skin lay open to the air.

The officer ordered his men to dispose of the two thieves.

"And the other?" one soldier asked.

"This is his mother," John said, pushing her forward.

"Ask of her," the officer said.

"Where do we take this one?"

Mary of Nazareth shook her head. "I have no place to bury him." She let out a loud wail and John pulled her close.

Jesus' body smacked the dirt with a loud thud as they dropped him at her feet causing the dust to fly around them.

Mary saw his muscles barely clinging to his back. She had never seen so deep into a human body. She never wanted to again.

Mary of Nazareth crawled to the body of her son and tried to turn him over. Mary came to her side along with John and the three of them were able to roll Jesus' body over onto his mother's lap. She pulled the body closer to her chest and rubbed his cheeks. She rocked him and held him like any mother would hold their child. She whispered a familiar lullaby in his ear.

The song made Mary miss her own mother who sang her the same song.

All around them, the crowd disbursed as if by command.

John reached over and pressed Jesus' eyelids closed.

Mary heard footsteps and looked up to see a figure approaching them with a scroll in his hand. "Joseph," she let his name flow over her tongue.

He handed the scroll to the centurion and said, "You will find everything in order."

The soldier opened the scroll with suspicion

and Mary watched his eyes dance over the papyrus. When he got to the end, he looked up at Joseph with raised eyebrows. "Pilate?"

Joseph nodded.

The centurion looked over the scroll again and then rolled it back up before placing it in his belt. "Take that body and follow this man," he ordered.

The guards nodded.

Joseph looked high in the sky and when his eyes slowly came down, they fell on Mary's face.

Mary tried to smile through the tears that filled her eyes, but it was a weak attempt.

Joseph's face remained solemn. He walked to the older woman's side and held his open palms out to her. "It's alright, Mother. Give him to me."

A scream erupted from her mouth. "No! Get away from me." Tears ran down her dusty cheeks.

Joseph looked deep into her eyes. "Look up at the sky, woman," he said and waited for her to obey.

The darkness still hung in the air, but it had cleared enough to see where the sun lay low in the sky.

"Sabbath is coming," he said. "I don't have much time."

She squeezed the bloody body against her chest and rocked him deeply. She sung in broken gasps into his ear.

Mary reached over and touched her shoulder. "Mother, it's time," she said. "We need to bury him before it's too late."

Her sobs slowed as she hugged Jesus deeply and wiped some blood from his face. She kissed his forehead and looked up into Joseph's waiting eyes. Nodding deeply, she released the body of her son.

The guards carefully picked up the body of Jesus and began to follow Joseph.

Mary helped John get Mary of Nazareth to her feet so that they could follow after the men.

"Mary," Mary of Nazareth whispered.

"Yes. I'm here." Mary grasped her outstretched hand.

"How much time do we have left?"

Mary searched the sky trying desperately to judge where the sun was before answering. "Not much, Mother, we'll have to move fast."

She nodded.

As they reached the bottom of the hill, Joseph turned around and put his hand up to stop them. "No."

Mary pleaded with her eyes first and then whispered, "Please, you have to let us go with you. He needs a proper burial."

Joseph looked into the sky with his dark eyes. "It's getting too late, we will not have enough time to get everything in order, but I have begun to make arrangements already. I'm sorry, but those plans do not include you."

Mary's lips quivered.

Joseph's eyes softened. "I didn't mean..." A sigh left his mouth. "I recently purchased a cave for myself, but Jesus needs it more than I do. It's ready. I am still alive to purchase another one. I couldn't stand to think of his body…"

Mary saw a shudder run through his entire body. She watched the two men carry Jesus' body out of sight. "I understand."

He turned his back on her and headed after his servants.

"I'm sorry, Joseph," Mary said to the wind. "But my plans don't include you either."

She turned to the group behind her. "John, can you go make sure we can stay in the room from last night? I'll make sure Mother is taken care of. We need to take a little walk in some fresh air."

John glanced down at Mary Nazareth, who was searching Mary's face.

Mary nodded slowly trying to communicate her plan without words.

She looked up at John and patted the hand he held her arm with. "I'll be fine."

"If you're sure."

"Yes. Take the others with you too," she said. "It's been a long day and they should finish preparing for Sabbath tomorrow."

"I'll go with you," Mary Magdalene said.

Mary nodded toward her friend. "Of course."

Joanna, Susanna, and Aunt Mary took their turns hugging Jesus' mother. "We'll see you soon," each promised.

When John and the other women's forms were out of sight, Mary pulled the remaining two women in closer. "Listen, we don't have much time. If we hurry, we can quietly follow Joseph to see where they are going to bury Jesus and get back in time for Sabbath."

The women nodded and each picked up the hem of their dresses to run. Silently, the three rushed after the group of men, but made sure they kept their distance so they would not be discovered.

After some time, Mary noticed the men enter a beautiful garden. She watched Joseph point to a cave and motioned for the men to drop the body off at the mouth. When they had placed Jesus' body down on the ground, the men turned and lined up against the side of the mountain.

Mary motioned for the women to follow her into a patch of trees to hide from the view of the men.

"Master, here are the items you requested," one of Joseph's servants spoke as he bent in half and waved to the small band of men that were placing jars, strips of cloth, and bowls on the ground next to the lifeless body.

"Thank you. Please, leave us. Take the men back home to prepare for Sabbath. I will join you." He looked up into the darkening sky. "As soon as I am able."

The man bowed again and then gathered the other servants before leaving.

Mary made her way a little closer and noticed that another man had been standing at the mouth of the cave holding a torch. She noticed his features. He was an older man and, by his garments, she could tell that he was of great importance.

As Joseph came close to the man, he greeted him, "Peace, Nicodemus."

"Peace," the man called back and returned the torch to its place on the outside of the cave.

"Did you bring what I asked?"

Nicodemus nodded. "I grabbed what I could. I'm afraid it's not much."

"I'm afraid we don't have much time anyway."

The two men bent low to the ground and began to pour aloes, myrrh, and rubbing spices into the strips of linen cloth before wrapping the body of Jesus. Starting at his toes, they worked their way up the body as swiftly as their hands could fly until they reached his shoulders.

The wind whipped up and brought the sweet scents to Mary's nose. She inhaled deeply and allowed the spices to work their relaxation powers over her tense body. Glancing up into the sky, she saw how late it was getting and hoped she would be able to get herself and the other women back inside the borrowed home in time.

When the men were satisfied with what they were able to do, they picked up Jesus' body and made their way into the cave.

Mary leaned back to where the other women hid behind her. "Stay here. I'll be right back," she said as she tiptoed to the opening of the cave.

She leaned as close as she dared without

allowing the men to see her. She saw them lay the body down on a shelf that had been hewn out of the rock.

Nicodemus laid a small cloth over Jesus' closed eyes and held it in place as Joseph wrapped a sheer cloth around the head.

Mary turned and ran as fast as she could back to the trees as the men made their way out of the dark cave.

A group of Roman soldiers came upon the men.

"We are here to seal the tomb," the officer said to Joseph.

"We are done and we'd be glad of the help." He patted the waiting boulder. "This is heavy."

All of the men gathered on one side of the rock and pushed it toward the mouth of the cave. With a loud thud, it fell into place.

"Seal it," the officer commanded.

Two guards stretched a red band across the stone and poured hot wax on both sides. With his ring, the officer pressed his mark into the wax as it dried.

After all the men had done what they were ordered to do, they left; the two Jewish men to observe Sabbath and the band of soldiers no doubt to celebrate.

Mary made her way over to the tomb leaving Jesus' mother and Mary Magdalene still hiding in the trees.

Stepping slowly up to the large rock, Mary

placed her hand on the cold, smooth stone. Her knees buckled under her causing her to fall down in front of the boulder that blocked her from the body of Jesus. She wept and allowed a loud wail to escape her mouth. Her entire body shook with sadness.

"I miss you," she whispered and stroked the stone. Rubbing her forehead against the boulder, she cried all the tears she could find.

Then she felt a hand on her shoulder. She turned to see the face of Mary Magdalene.

"Mother says we need to go."

Mary nodded up at her friend as she slowly rose to her feet.

The two hung on to each other as they collected Mary of Nazareth and made their way back toward the city.

Mary wanted to be with her friends, she wanted to help take care of those whom she had taken care of for the last several months. She longed for their comfort and to be a comfort to them. Yet, the biggest part of her wanted nothing more than to lie at the tomb and weep until there was nothing left of her but wet sand at the foot of the large stone.

At The Twelfth Hour

"And now when the even was come, because it was the preparation, that is, the day before the sabbath,"
-MARK 15:42

Jerusalem, 6 PM

The women made it to the house just in time.

John was there speaking with the owner when they entered. He gave them a slight nod as they passed deeper into the home to find the other women.

"Mary." Joanna hugged her as they came into the courtyard. "I'm so glad you're safe. We heard the Romans were out in search tonight."

"We saw them in the streets," Mary of Nazareth said.

"Everything is stirred tonight," Susanna said.

"Have we heard from any of the other men yet?" Mary asked.

Joanna shook her head. "John's worried."

"He's afraid they might have been captured," Susanna added.

"We would have received word if they had been," Mary of Nazareth comforted.

"Come," Joanna said. "We have some food for you. You must be hungry."

The women sat in one of the side rooms and enjoyed a small meal together.

As night grew deeper outside, a knock was heard at the door.

John waved the owner of the house back. "I'll go."

Mary heard murmured voices at the front door for some time before footsteps made their way toward the room.

"James," Joanna rushed him.

The young man blushed under her embrace.

"Come, brother," John said with a hand on his shoulder. "Let's get you some food."

"Joanna, you need to watch yourself," Susanna scolded.

"Forgive me," she said with a duck of her head. "I was just so happy to see him alive."

The women huddled together on the dirty floor.

Mary's eyes were heavy. The events of the past few days weighed on her. As the breathing around her slowed to a smooth, steady beat, the undertow of sleep pulled on her. She closed her eyes and let it overtake her.

It wasn't too long before knocking roused her. She heard rustling in the courtyard and rose to see what the commotion was.

"Matthew. James bar-Alpheus. Bartholomew."

"Greetings, Mary," the men said.

"I'm happy to see you all are well. There is fruit and bread in the kitchen if you're hungry."

"The other men are upstairs," John said.

The three tired men dragged themselves up the stairs, but not before each grabbed a handful of food to take with them.

"Do you think the rest will arrive?" Mary asked John when the men had cleared the last step.

"I didn't know these would."

A knock at the door interrupted them.

Mary followed close behind John.

At the door was Philip.

"Please, come in." John waved him inside.

"Help yourself to food," Mary said. "Then head upstairs and get some sleep."

"That's almost everyone," John said.

"Almost."

John went into the kitchen and broke a piece of bread. He tossed the piece in his mouth and then tore another chunk and handed it to Mary.

She took it and ate it. The shallow lines around John's eyes appeared. "You're worried."

John nodded. "Just thinking about Peter."

"What?"

"You didn't hear?"

Mary shook her head.

He leaned on the table. "Before I came to find you women at the hill, I had been to the courtyard of Caiaphas, the High Priest. I was trying to find

Peter who had been let in during the trial. I had to wait outside, but he never came back out. I had searched a few other places before returning." Rubbing his stubble, he continued, "They were talking about all the things that were unfolding. Some of them were discussing Peter."

"What were they saying?"

"It happened just the way Jesus said." He shook his head with a grin. "Exactly the way he said."

Mary nodded. It didn't surprise her that something happened the exact way Jesus had predicted. He was always right.

"He told Peter that before the cock crew, Peter would deny him three times. It happened. They were saying Peter had denied even knowing Jesus, much less following him. They said the rooster crowed and then Peter went running away. No one has seen him since."

"Poor Peter."

A deep pounding at the back end of the courtyard made Mary jump.

John went to open the door.

Two men rushed in.

"Peter!" Mary gasped.

The leader stopped short of the woman and took a deep breath. "Shut the door!"

John obeyed.

"Andrew," Mary said as he came near. "Why are the two of you out of breath?"

"We were running away from some guards,"

he said over short breaths.

"We had to race through the back streets in order to lose them."

"John," Peter called. "Where are the rest?"

"Peace," John said. "They are upstairs sleeping."

"And the women are in the other room sleeping as well," Mary offered.

"All?" Peter asked.

John took a quick count in his head. "No."

"No?" Andrew asked.

"Thomas. He has yet to show. And we haven't seen Thaddeus or Simon either."

"We met Thomas," Andrew said. "But he didn't want to come with us."

"Then that is all."

"You're sure?" Peter demanded.

John reconsidered. "With the exception of…"

"Who?" Peter asked.

"Judas Iscariot."

"That snake!" Andrew spat and rushed toward John.

"Peace," Peter said and put his hands on his brother's chest.

"Don't mention that name in my presence again."

"Mary, why don't you go back to sleep," John said. He took her elbow and turned her toward the side room. "We should all get some rest. I'll see them upstairs."

Mary nodded and obeyed. She knew the men

needed each other and some space. She knew she desperately needed sleep.

At The Borrowed House

> *"And the veil of the temple was rent in twain*
> *from the top to the bottom."*
> -MARK 15:38

Saturday Morning

Mary rolled over on the dirt floor and opened her eyes to see the bodies of the women she had spent yesterday with, lying around her. The men were still sleeping upstairs. The owner of the home had graciously agreed to allow all of them to stay as long as they needed. He cared for Jesus and wanted to honor him, even in death.

Mary of Nazareth was standing across the room with her back to Mary. She could tell the older woman was in the middle of preparing something to eat. She watched her well-trained hands flow from platter to platter. The woman's aging feet barely moved from their spot in front of the table she was working at while her upper body moved back and forth like an olive branch in the wind, bending ever so slightly while the base and roots stood firm.

Quietly Mary rose and went to her.

She turned just as Mary made her way to her side and smiled. Though time had worn and wrinkled her face, there was so much light in her eyes.

He had her eyes. The thought made Mary turn her head as the tears threatened to burn their way out of her eyes. Thankfully, she turned her gaze back to the task at her hands while Mary was able to take a deep breath to steady her pounding heart.

Mary looked back at her and studied her face. She remembered her as the beautiful young woman she had met many years ago. She was still beautiful standing before her now, but her skin held the well-earned marks of years standing over a fire and chasing children around. She could see the smooth olive complexion shine through the leather that replaced it. Her lips were a perfect shape and her nose was perfectly portioned with her face. Mary chuckled to herself, remembering how much Martha had complained when they were young about her nose. Their family tended to grow them quite large and her sister had always considered hers too big for her face. She missed Martha.

Mary of Nazareth looked back up at Mary and said, "No tears. Remember, no mourning on the Sabbath." She was calm, but Mary noticed the tears soaking her eyes as well. She couldn't imagine the pain that was lying just below the surface of the woman's composure.

Mary had lost family members, so she could sympathize to a point, but never a child. Nothing could be so great a pain as to bury a body that once lived inside you for almost a year. A body that you had spent your whole life protecting and teaching. Then to watch that body be tortured and hastily buried in a strange tomb without being able to observe proper ritual. Her poor heart must be breaking into a countless number of pieces. Yet, here she stood getting food ready for all the bodies, that she did not give birth to sprawled around her.

Mary admired her strength. It had been something she had searched for all her life and now saw it displayed before her.

As if Mary of Nazareth could hear her thoughts, she motioned to a large bowl.

Mary nodded and began to help.

It wasn't long before the smell of food caused the entire house to stir with activity. With all the women and most of the men crammed into the one house, the walls seemed like they would burst with the overflow of bodies.

Mary let the silence hang around. She was content to listen to the others fill the void with words.

"Do you think we should go to the Temple today?" Susanna asked.

Mary watched the question race across the faces of the other women in the circle before she answered, "I don't know."

The men had also fallen silent with the question.

Looking over at John, Mary lifted her eyebrows with the question.

"It might not be a bad idea." John cleared his throat. "It would get us out for a little while."

"Do you think it will be safe out in the city?" Mary of Nazareth asked.

"I'm sure things have calmed down," Andrew answered. "Even the shakes are lessening in intensity from the earthquake yesterday."

John nodded. "We'll go to the Temple."

When everyone had finished their meal, they began to prepare themselves.

John stopped his newly adopted mother at the front door. "Whatever happens, stay close to me."

Mary of Nazareth nodded and held onto his extended arm.

With the added stress of yesterday, Mother looked older today than she had in all the years Mary had known her.

Taking their time, the group slowly made its way toward the massive Temple. Andrew led the way for the group. His eyes searching the streets for any potential danger. Peter took up the rear. Mary had seen the once fearless leader reduced to a humiliated dog holding his tail between his legs. She thought about what John had told her of Peter's denial of Jesus in Caiaphas' courtyard. The guilt weighed on him like a heavy yoke.

Though it was the Sabbath and most families

would be spending much of the day inside, there was the occasional body that passed by as they walked the dusty streets. It was still early enough that not many families were coming to the Temple yet. The group was able to make their way without trouble.

When they reached the Temple, John drew Mary of Nazareth close to himself. Mary's eyes flew to the large ornate building in front of them.

As they ascended the grand staircase that led to the first open courtyard, Andrew ran over to a man who was standing among a group of men. "Simon," he called out.

"Andrew," the man replied as he turned his attention to the man running towards him.

The two embraced and talked before Andrew came back toward the group. They had Thaddeus with them too.

"Have you heard what happened inside?" Simon asked as they approached the group.

Andrew shook his head slightly.

"The inner Temple is partially destroyed."

"And the veil," Thaddeus interrupted. "Tell them about the veil."

Mary looked back and forth between the men.

"Yes, we went inside earlier," Simon said. "You can clearly see the large curtain that separated the Holy of Holies from our sight is hanging in two pieces as if it had been ripped from top to bottom."

"That's impossible," Peter remarked.

Simon answered, "I know. It shouldn't be, but it's there. You can see it for yourself. We can look directly into the Holy place."

"That curtain was half a cubit thick," Peter said. "How could it be ripped down the middle?"

"Go see for yourself." Thaddeus pointed toward the inner courtyard.

John stepped forward, but Mary of Nazareth pulled on his arm. He turned back toward her and patted her hand like one would do to a worried child. "It's alright, Mother, I'm just going to go take a look then I'll be right back." John glanced over at Mary. "Here," he said, as he removed her hand from his arm and held it out to Mary. "Stay here with Mary. You'll be fine."

Mary took the woman's hand and held it with both of hers.

Mother nodded at John.

All the men rushed off toward the inner courtyard while Mary stood with the women just outside the outer courtyard. They found a clear corner in the court of women and sat in a circle. Each kept their eyes on the gates that led deep inside the Temple.

Mary let her eyes fall to a familiar side room. The place Jesus liked to sit and teach. "I miss him so much," the thought escaped her lips just above a whisper.

"Me too," Jesus' mother agreed.

"I just can't believe he's really gone," Mary's voice cracked with the sorrow.

The older woman nodded and said, "It's alright. Come here, sweet child." She pulled her in close to a loving embrace. "I want to share something with you that my mother used to tell me. We are all like little needles running around this world with invisible threads behind us that are our lives. When we meet people, and they become part of our life, our threads get entwined with theirs. Some are forever, but some are only temporarily tied to us. When we look around, all we see are the knots, loose hanging threads, empty spaces, and broken ties that seem to make a big mess. Yet, when God looks down on us, He sees the beautiful masterpiece that He is weaving together."

Mary looked up into her dark eyes as hers began to dry.

"You see. It's like we are looking up and all we see is the underside of a woven rug, but God is looking down on us and He sees the beautiful pattern He is creating." She pointed up to emphasize her point. "So even though it feels like chaos sometimes, just remember that God is the one in control of the masterpiece. You just have to let him pull the thread of your life in His order."

They held onto each other for a while in the silence. The courtyard was filling up, but no one came to them. Devout Jews were coming to fulfill their religious obligations and beg for the mercy of a powerful God. Many men came out of the inner courts deep in discussion with each other.

Priests arrived and were directing them away from the center of the Temple. Many hung around the courtyard of women trying to find an explanation for the unveiling of the Holy of Holies.

Mary leaned out of Mary of Nazareth's arms to stretch her neck toward the gate the men had gone through. She looked back at the older woman who had a sweet sadness in her eyes.

"I remember when I first brought Jesus here. He was such a tiny little thing." She chuckled to herself as she looked down and held her arms together in front of her like she was holding a baby. Rocking her arms back and forth a few times, she sighed and then wrapped them around herself. "Of course, I was so young back then too." Her smile returned briefly as she looked up into Mary's eyes.

Mary smiled back. "Will you tell me about him? I mean as a baby."

She nodded. "I remember everything about him from the moment the..." she trailed off with concern in her voice.

"The what?"

She chuckled to herself a little more. "Seems kind of fitting now."

Mary tilted her head to the side.

"I haven't really shared the details of Jesus' birth with a lot of people beyond my husband, Joseph."

"You must miss Joseph," Mary said without thinking.

"Oh, yes. He was sick for a long time and stayed so strong for us, but eventually, it overtook his body and he passed away."

"I'm sorry. I didn't mean to add to your pain."

"Don't be," she said, patting Mary's folded hands. "He was such a good man. I was fortunate to be married to such an amazingly understanding man. He was sweet and so good with all the kids.

"When I was a very young woman, an angel of the Lord came to me. He said, 'Do not fear. You have found favor with God and you will conceive in your womb and bring forth a son. You will call his name Jesus. He will be great and will be called the Son of the Highest. The Lord God will give him the throne of his father David. He will reign over the house of Jacob forever and his kingdom will not have an end.'"

"An angel told you this?" Mary scrunched her forehead, trying to imagine the story.

"Yes. I asked him how it was at all possible because I was a virgin and had not known my betrothed."

"What did he say?"

She laughed to herself. "He said 'The Holy Ghost will come upon you and the power of the Highest will overshadow you. Therefore, the holy thing which will be born of you will be called the Son of God.'"

"And you believed him?"

"When an angel shows up, you believe him. Trust me," she said. "Then he went on and added a detail to make sure I trusted the message."

"What?"

"He told me that my cousin, Elizabeth, was going to give birth to a son."

"That doesn't seem too outrageous to believe."

"Elizabeth was well past the age to bear a child, even though she had prayed for a son for as long as I can remember." Mary adjusted her headpiece. "The angel even told me that she was exactly in her sixth month of pregnancy."

"Was that all he said?"

She closed her eyes. "He said one more thing that has always stuck with me." She opened her eyes and looked directly at Mary. "He said, 'With God, nothing will be impossible.'"

Mary thought on the message.

"Of course, me being so young, none of it made any sense. I guess, with God, sometimes things don't make much sense and that is just His way of showing Himself to be behind it all."

Mary nodded, remembering all Jesus had done for her. Some of it didn't make sense, but all of it had brought God glory and her closer to the divine than she had ever been.

"After the angel left, I packed a bag and went rushing off to see my cousin," she continued. "I had to see for myself if what the angel had told me was true. I also needed to tell someone who would actually believe me about the things the angel said were going to happen."

"Did she believe you?"

The older woman shifted her legs and folded her hands in her lap. "Yes, she did. The moment I came upon her, she told me that the baby growing inside her leaped at the sound of my voice. I was so relieved that she not only believed me, but that God was smoothing out the way before me to show me that what He had said through his messenger was true."

"Did you tell your parents?"

She looked down beside herself. "I stayed with Elizabeth for a few months before heading home. I wish I would have stayed with her longer, but I was beginning to show and didn't want word to race ahead of me. I hadn't told my parents before I left. When I got back home, I tried to talk to them a few times. At first, they brushed me and my words off as ramblings. It wasn't long before I was showing enough that they had to believe me." She rubbed her flat stomach. "It was pretty hard to ignore once I grew out of my dresses.

"That's when life got difficult. They wouldn't let me out of the house. My mother and father repeatedly questioned me about what I had done to dishonor myself. They wouldn't let me see Joseph."

Mary felt her heartache.

"Elizabeth was so proud of John. She wrote to me all the time about how he was growing. Eventually, the letters stopped. When we visited Jerusalem that last time, we found out that both Zachariah and Elizabeth had died. We begged the priests to let us take John. He needed to be around family. They denied us. Instead, they sent him out to the desert with those extremists."

"But God did use him," Mary said. "He led many to God and even baptized Jesus. He told everyone that they needed to follow Jesus because he was the lamb that God had sent into the world."

She got quiet for a few moments before she looked up. There were fresh tears in her eyes when she spoke, "And look where it got both of them. John was beheaded for speaking out against Herod. And my baby was…"

"I'm sorry."

"Jesus took John's death the hardest. They were like brothers." She took a deep breath. "But I'm getting ahead of myself. Where was I?"

"You were telling me about being pregnant."

"Right. When I was very heavy with him, Joseph received word that we had to travel to Bethlehem to be counted and taxed."

"The Roman's love their numbers." Mary shook her head.

"Yes, they do. It was a hard journey, but we made it just in time for me to deliver. In a watchtower."

"A watchtower?"

She nodded. "By the time we were able to make it into the city, it was overflowing with people. The Innkeeper pointed us in the direction of a nearby watchtower, Migdal Eder. It was the place where shepherds took their pregnant sheep to give birth to the lambs who would be used as sacrifices. It was warm and soft with hay. Not the most ideal place for a human to give birth, mind you, but it was far better than out in the wilderness. After I wrapped him up in a piece of cloth, these shepherds came out of nowhere to worship him. It was so much for me to take in all at once."

"Shepherds?"

"Yes, they told us angels had appeared to them in the night sky and told them where to find us. They were familiar with the watchtower, having used it on several occasions for their own flocks."

"That's strange."

"When I had carefully observed my time of cleansing, we brought Jesus here to be dedicated to the Lord. Not one, but two different people came to us and told us miraculous things.

"The first was an old man by the name of Simon. He came over and blessed us. He said, 'This child is destined to cause many in Israel to fall, and many others to rise. He has been sent as a sign from God, but many will oppose him. As a result, the deepest thoughts of many hearts will be revealed. And a sword will pierce your very soul.' It was so unnerving to hear that the infant son in my arms would one day reveal the hearts of others.

"The second was an older woman named Anna. She was a prophetess in the Temple who hadn't left since her husband died over sixty years before. She came over to us while Simon was talking and started singing praises to God. She was worshipping Jesus as if God had stepped down into human form. It was as if her eyes were seeing the invisible God she had spent decades praying to."

Mary remembered Jesus' face. It was overwhelming for her to think of the face of God being so humble and real.

"Do you remember when we visited your family with Jesus for the first time?"

The flood of blood-stained memories peaked in Mary's mind. She shuttered and pushed them away. "I remember what happened when you left."

Mother gasped. "You don't remember the ones who studied the stars and their gifts?"

Mary shook her head.

"Well, you were very young. As we stayed with your family, a knock came at the door one night. When Joseph answered it, a group of ornately dressed men came in. They were highly respected men who spent their lives studying the star. They had received a sign in the heavens that told them about Jesus. They had gifts for him."

"Gifts?"

"Gold, Frankincense, and Myrrh. Your father offered to keep the spices safe for us when we had to flee. You don't remember how they worshipped Jesus?"

Short bursts of faces and colors danced in her mind's eye.

"After we visited your family," she continued.

"We were instructed to hide down in Egypt for a few years. When Herod passed away, we headed home."

Mary choked back the fear and sorrow of the past.

Mother's eyes moistened. "He was an amazing child."

"Do you know what happened when you left?"

Mother hid her face.

"They came for him," Mary's voice wavered. "The Romans. They invaded our homes, bringing fear and hate with them. They spent the entire night searching every house and ripping babies out of their mother's arms." Tears burned her eyes and warmed her cheeks. "So much innocent blood stained our streets. It was months before the rains washed it all away." Mary ducked her head and began to weep.

"Child." The older woman wrapped her arms around Mary's shoulders. "I'm sorry." When Mary's cries subsided, Jesus' mother asked, "Do you remember when he was about twelve?"

Mary wiped her wet face with her sleeve and nodded.

"We traveled with much of our extended family and friends to this very temple to observe the Passover. When the feast was over, we headed back home. We got about halfway along the journey when we couldn't find Jesus among the group."

"I remember. Martha and I found him in the

Temple teaching to a group of leaders."

"Teaching, was he?"

"Yes, we had interrupted when we came upon him."

"I remember him saying something about doing his father's business, but it never made any sense to me. Until later. He was speaking as God being his father. It makes sense now. The angel told me that the baby conceived in me was from God, so that would make Him Jesus' father."

They let a pause hang between them.

"Joseph was so upset when we couldn't find Jesus," Mary of Nazareth said. "I guess now I can understand why."

Mary raised her eyebrow at the older woman.

"Could you imagine having to explain to God that we had lost His son?" She let out a belly laugh.

Mary laughed too.

Mary of Nazareth quieted and then began to sob. "I miss him so much."

Mary hugged her until they both had no more tears to cry. Wiping her eyes, she caught sight of John coming through the gate.

The women rose as he came close.

"It's true, all of it," John began. "Yesterday, at the same time as the great earthquake during the sacrifices, the priests recorded that the veil, which blocked the Holy of Holies from view, was torn straight down from top to bottom. They have been scrambling ever since to try to repair it to no avail. Sacrifices and offerings are still being performed and the priests are pressuring the weak-minded into bringing more to appease God. They are giving the explanation that the events that happened are because we have not taken this Passover seriously and God is showing us His anger."

"That's not true," Mary of Nazareth said.

"We know that," John answered.

"I don't like any of this," Simon spoke up.

"Neither do I," John agreed. "I think it best that we head back to the house. I don't like the way things are progressing here in the city. People are scared and it's easier to make irrational decisions in that state of mind."

"Word has already reached us here about Barabbas," Thaddeus said. "He has picked up where he left off when he was taken away in chains the first time. It will only be a matter of time before he spills blood on the streets in the name of his cause."

At The Cellar

*"And they returned, and prepared spices and
ointments; and rested the sabbath day according
to the commandment."*
-LUKE 23:56

Saturday, Midday

Each of the six women and ten men found
themselves a spot in the open courtyard of the
borrowed house. Many took bits of food or sat in
deep thought, but no one said a word. The silence
hung over them like a heavy curtain.

After hours of silence, Mary feared she would
start screaming. It had been a long time since she
had been confined in a house with so many people.
Even during those times, she had Jesus and his
teachings to distract her. The sound of so many
bodies breathing was enough to raise her
uneasiness. She couldn't take much more without
going completely insane. She had to leave and
soon.

She stood and found Mary of Nazareth in the
kitchen. "I'm going out for a while. I'll be back

before nightfall."

"But, it's the Sabbath. And the whole city is stirred with bloodlust. I don't think it's a good idea."

"I know I should stay, but I really need some fresh air. God will forgive my wanderings today. I just can't sit here anymore."

"I think you should stay too," John said, overhearing their whispers.

She turned toward him. "I understand the concern, but I know how to take care of myself. I know these streets better than most. I'll hide my face and make it out of the gates without any Roman guards seeing me. I need to go check on my family. I promise to be back before the gates close for the night."

John sighed. "I can't make you stay."

"Nothing can keep me away either. I promise to stay safe."

John reluctantly nodded.

"Here." Mother handed her a small satchel. "Go see your family."

"Thank you." She took the bag, kissed the woman's cheek, and headed out the back door.

Lifting her scarf, Mary carefully adjusted it over her head and wrapped one of the bottom pieces over her mouth and nose. Then she raised the strap of the bag over her head so the bag would hang across her body. This would leave her hands free. She took a deep breath and made her way through the back streets heading for the city gates.

She made it to the last buildings when someone grabbed her arm. She spun around to meet the armored chest of a sizeable Roman soldier. His grip tightened around her forearm.

"Where do you think you're going?" he barked.

"Pardon me, sir." She sang in a high voice that she had not used in some time. "I am but a stranger in your land."

"You look very familiar," he said and pulled her in close.

She could smell the strong drink on his breath. "Forgive me, please. I was trying to go home. Your city has had much chaos and I wanted to leave."

"Just where is your home?"

"Magdala," she said with little thought. She prayed Mary Magdalene would forgive her for borrowing her hometown for her lie.

"Magdala, huh?" He pulled her up to her tiptoes so he could look into her eyes. "Are you that Mary woman who followed that crazy teacher?"

"No, good soldier." She smiled bright, hoping it would turn her eyes gentle and pass as the truth. "My name is Eila." She chided herself inwardly, but knew her mother wouldn't mind her borrowed name to escape certain death. "I came to visit friends, but with all your region's trouble, I find it best if I see myself home."

He looked her over before setting her down. "See to it that you do. And quickly."

"Thank you, sir." Once he released her arm, she bowed deeply and hastened through the gate. She ran a reasonable distance before she slowed her pace and could take a deep breath.

It wasn't long before she came upon the familiar childhood home in Bethany that she knew so well.

"Lazarus? Martha?" she called into the courtyard. "It's me."

"Mary?" Lazarus rushed toward her and enclosed her in an embrace. "Sister, it is so good to see you are well."

She hugged him tight. "Brother, I have missed you."

"Mary," Martha called from the entrance to the kitchen. "Bless my eyes." She ran to kiss her cheeks. "We've heard just awful things happening in Jerusalem."

"They are true."

"All of it?" Lazarus asked.

"Yes."

"The veil in the Temple?" Martha asked.

"Yes. Oh, I have much to tell, but I must be quick. I promised John I'd be back before nightfall."

"Back?" Lazarus asked. "You can't go back."

"Yes, I am. They need me."

"Mary, you shouldn't have even been traveling on the Sabbath," Martha scolded. "You need to stay here."

"I need to be there with them."

"And what of us?" Lazarus asked.

"You'll be safe as long as you stay here. The Romans don't care about you anymore. They have won. Jesus is dead and buried and we are all in hiding until their rage fully subsides."

"I forbid you to return to Jerusalem," Lazarus commanded. "This night or any other night."

"Forgive me, brother, but you have no right to forbid me from doing anything," Mary corrected. When she saw the pain fill his eyes, she softened. "Forgive me. I didn't mean it like that. I know you are supposed to be Martha and I's protector, but it had been such a long time that we took care of you. It was almost as if you were a son to us instead of a brother."

"That's true," Martha agreed.

"Brother." She put a hand on his shoulder. "I know what God has called me to do. Though it took a long time, I'm finally listening. Please don't make me break your heart by obeying God over you. I will choose Him every time. I lived far too long away from His path to give it up now."

Lazarus looked deep into her eyes. "I just want you safe."

"I know." She hugged him. "I would rather be in danger in God's will than safe in my own."

Martha wiped a tear away from her eye with her hand cloth.

"I can stay for a little bit, but then I must leave. I have so much to tell you both."

"Let's hear it then," Lazarus said.

It was late in the afternoon when Mary prepared to leave her siblings. "There is one more thing I need to do before I go," she said and took the steps that led down to her father's storage room.

She searched the back corner shelves and found what she sought. Two bottles sat alone on an upper ledge. They were covered with dust, but Mary knew they were what she wanted. Hastily, she placed them in her bag and went back upstairs to kiss her brother and sister goodbye.

She promised to do everything in her power to stay safe and return to them again as quickly as she could. Though she couldn't promise when that would be exactly, she left them with love and blessings.

As Mary walked the worn path back to Jerusalem, she tried to focus on the land around her, but everything ended up reminding her of Jesus.

The rolling hillside reminded her of his craftsman's muscles that rolled along his arms and back. The smooth ground laid out before her reminded her of his smooth olive skin. Even the sweet, earthy air that blew against her face reminded her of his sweet scent when she got the rare opportunity to be close to him.

Mary began to cry and started to run, trying to

get away from the overwhelming sense that something had taken a large hole out of the middle of her very soul.

When her legs burned with fatigue, she slowed her pace to a walk. She neared the city gate and quietly entered. Doing her best to avoid anyone, she made her way through the back streets to reach the borrowed house. She doubled back in order to make sure no one was following her before she let herself in through the back door of the house.

Without finding any of the women or reporting to any of the men. Mary found a quiet spot in one of the side rooms. She laid down and wept herself to sleep. Jesus' face was all she could think about.

Later, Mary of Nazareth came in to check on her.

Mary sat up and hugged the woman. "I'm sorry. I should have checked in when I got back. I was just so tired."

"I understand. We've all been through so much more than any one person should bear."

A thought entered Mary's mind and she reached for the borrowed bag. "Here," she said, placing it in her lap. "For you."

"Thank you for returning this."

"No. Look inside." Mary pointed. "I brought you something."

"For me?" the older woman asked as she opened the bag. "What could it be?" She lifted the first dusty bottle and held it up.

Mary saw the water fill her eyes. "I found the Frankincense and Myrrh you talked about while at my house. I remembered where Father kept them."

"I can't accept these." Mother put the bottle back in the bag and pushed it to Mary.

"I'm not giving them to you. I'm returning them. They belong to you."

"They belong to him," she said quietly.

"Then maybe we can return them," Mary Magdalene said over Mary of Nazareth's shoulder.

They both turned to her.

"I was thinking about last night." She sat in front of the women. "How you told me that Jesus didn't get a proper burial by your people's customs."

Jesus' mother nodded slowly.

"And I know today was a time to observe your Sabbath rest."

Again, she nodded, trying to find Mary Magdalene's thought path.

"I was wondering if we could go in the morning and give him a proper burial. You know, as a way to honor him."

Mary of Nazareth reached over and hugged the woman. "Thank you," she whispered into her dark, curly hair. "And thank you," she pulled Mary in. "Now, we have the spices with which complete our task."

"It's settled then," Mary Magdalene said. "At

first light, we'll head to the tomb."

At The Dawn

"Now upon the first day of the week, very early in the morning, they came unto the sepulchre, bringing the spices which they had prepared, and certain others with them."
-LUKE 24:1

Sunday Morning

Mary watched the fleeing darkness outside for as long as she could through the open window. The night had brought many nightmares making sleep impossible for her. Between the images of Jesus' body hanging from the cross and the thought of unwrapping his dead body, her mind played evil tricks on her through the long hours.

She remembered the sight of Lazarus walking out of his tomb and the fresh, clean skin that was discovered as the men unwrapped him from his burial linens. Such would not be discovered upon unwrapping Jesus.

Her heart tore in two. It matched the great divide in her soul. She wanted very much to look on Jesus once more, but she didn't know if her sanity could handle anymore.

She didn't want to go to the tomb because she had already anointed his body for burial. She couldn't stand the thought of laying eyes on his corpse again. The agony on his face, the strips of flesh dangling from his body, all of it came flooding back to her. She rolled over onto her side, pulled her knees up to her chest, and began to weep.

"Mary?" someone whispered. Mary Magdalene was by her side in a moment. "Are you ill?"

"I can't do it," she said over sobs. "I just can't see him like that again."

"Oh," Mary Magdalene said. "I see. I didn't think about that last night when I offered."

Mary sat up. "I can't tell you how much I appreciate your care for us and for the ways of our people." She rubbed her eyes. "Take Mother. Ask the others if they want to go as well. I just can't-" her voice betrayed her again.

Mary Magdalene brushed her fingers through Mary's hair. "There now. Don't weep so. I'm sure Mother will understand. She was very grateful for your gift."

Mary nodded. "I'll help you get everything ready."

The two woke the other women. Together they hurriedly prepared some clean strips of linen and readied everything they would need.

"We'll return soon," Mary Magdalene

promised as they left Mary in the house alone with the still sleeping men.

When the sun shone through the open windows and the men were beginning to stir upstairs, Mary heard someone come through the front door. She hurried to see the women enter. They all had flushed cheeks and short breaths. "What happened?"

"You wouldn't believe us," Mary of Nazareth started. She sat down and leaned against a wooden support.

"It's all too wonderful," Joanna said.

"What is?" Mary came near to them.

"I still can't believe my own eyes," Susanna said.

"Will someone please tell me what has gotten all of you so worked up?" Mary insisted.

Mary of Nazareth shook her head. "The tomb is-"

"Mary!" Mary Magdalene rushed through the open door.

"Peace, sister." Mary reached for the woman. "Can you please tell me what happened at the tomb?"

"We were getting close the garden," Mary Magdalene said over gasps. "We slowed down because Mother and I realized we didn't plan on who would help us move the stone."

The other woman nodded.

"We thought about sending Joanna and Susanna back to fetch some of the men."

"That's when we also remembered the guard and seal that had been placed on the tomb," Mary of Nazareth said. "There was no way the soldiers were going to let us break the seal. Such an act is punishable by death."

"We didn't know what to do," Joanna said.

"That's right," Mary Magdalene picked up. "We just stood there, trying to think of a plan."

"And then?" Mary asked.

"And then," Mary Magdalene said, with a great wave of her hand. "The ground under our feet began to shake. It shook like at the cross."

"Just like it," Susanna agreed.

"We grabbed hold of each other and hung on until it stopped."

"It almost knocked us clear off our feet," Mary of Nazareth said.

"When the shaking stopped," Mary Magdalene continued. "We ran closer to see the tomb. And-"

"The stone was rolled away!" Joanna said.

"What?"

"It's true," Mary Magdalene said. "The mouth of the tomb was open. The seal lay on the ground and the large stone was off to the side."

"I don't believe it."

"I speak truth." Mary Magdalene put her hands on her hips in defense. "They saw it too." She waved a hand around to the other women who all nodded their heads in agreement. "Then we saw the soldiers running toward us."

"We thought they were coming to arrest us," Susanna said.

"But they ran right past us and off into the horizon," Joanna added.

"They looked as ashen as dead men," Mary of Nazareth said.

"What had frightened them so?" Mary asked. "Surely it would have taken more than an earthquake to put that kind of fear into trained Roman soldiers."

"We were about to find out," Mary Magdalene said. "But first we didn't know if they had moved the stone or if the earthquake shook it loose, but it was moved and they were gone. We were going to take our chances and anoint Jesus' body."

"The two of them headed to the cave while Joanna and myself headed back here to get the men," Susanna said.

"Mother and I got near the tomb when we saw the brightest light I have ever seen," Mary Magdalene said.

"I had to cover my eyes it was so bright," Mary of Nazareth agreed.

"A man dressed in pure white was sitting on top of the stone looking down on us," Mary Magdalene continued. "We both hit our knees and bowed our foreheads to the ground. I understood why the soldiers had run away. The man was emanating the holiness of God. They couldn't stand to be in his presence."

"He looked a lot like the angel who had visited

me," Mary of Nazareth said. "The one who told me I would give birth to Jesus."

"He was so beautiful. His entire body glowed with a light that I would have mistaken for the noonday sun if I wasn't sure it was still hiding in the early morning hours."

"What did he say?" Mary asked.

"He asked us why we were seeking the living among the dead," Mary of Nazareth answered.

"He told us not to fear," Mary Magdalene recounted. "He knew we were looking for Jesus, but Jesus was no longer in the tomb."

"Then where was he?" Mary asked.

"Not there," Mary Magdalene said, with deep sorrow evident in her voice.

"It's true," Mary of Nazareth said. She rose to her feet. "He told us to go into the open tomb and see for ourselves that his body was no longer there."

"Did you?" Mary asked.

Mary Magdalene nodded slowly. "We went inside and looked around. There was no body, but the burial clothes lay right where the men had placed him."

"When we stepped back outside," Mary of Nazareth said. "The angel told us to come back here and tell the men what we saw. And that they should go back to Galilee and wait for him there."

"What is all the commotion?" John said from the upper room.

"Go and see," Mary Magdalene called up to

him. "Jesus is no longer in the tomb."

"What?" Peter asked, rushing down the stairs.

"Go and see!" Joanna said.

"They have taken away our Lord. We don't know who or where they took him," Mary Magdalene pleaded.

John and Peter ran out of the house.

Mary Magdalene ran after them.

"She is quite upset," Mother said to Mary. "She thinks someone took his body during the earthquake."

"What is going on down here," Simon asked as he entered the courtyard followed by many of the other men.

"These women have been telling us of their trip to the tomb," Mary said. "John and Peter just rushed out to see for themselves."

The men huddled together with whispers of theories and concern over the recounted witness of the women.

It wasn't long before Peter and John returned to validate everything the women had told them.

"It was like they said," Peter said.

"Right down to the burial clothes," John said. "The strip that covered his eyes was folded and set apart from the other linens."

Behind them, Mary Magdalene ran into the courtyard. "I've seen him!" she shouted and spun around the room.

"Who?" Mary asked.

"Master, I've seen him. He is risen just as he

said," she sang and began to twirl around the room.

"Jesus?"

"Yes!"

"Speak on, woman," John said.

"I followed you men to the tomb. I needed to see for myself again. It broke my heart to think that his body wasn't where it was supposed to be. I needed to find out what happened." She took a breath. "When the men left, I went back to the mouth of the cave. I bent down and looked inside. It was just as empty as when I had seen it the first time. It drove me to my knees and I sat there weeping. The angel who spoke to me and Mother was gone, but two others sat on the ledge where his body had been. One at the head and one at the feet.

"They looked at me and one asked why I was crying. I told them I wanted to know where the body of Jesus was and I didn't know who took him away. They didn't answer me, so I turned my back on them.

"A man was standing nearby and he also asked me why I was crying. I thought he might have been the keeper of the garden, so I asked him where he had taken the body. I thought maybe he moved the body because the tomb might have been damaged by the earthquake, so he needed to secure the body. I asked him to take me to Jesus. And then he…"

"He what?" Mary stepped closer to her friend.

Mary Magdalene's eyes grew large. "He said my name." Tears spilled out onto her cheeks. "It was Master. I recognized his voice."

"You're sure it was him?" John inquired.

"I'd stake my life on it." She turned back to Mary. "I hugged him so tight. I never wanted to let go. I couldn't believe he was standing there, right in front of me."

"What did he say?" Mary asked.

"After a few moments, he asked me to let him go." She chuckled. "I guess he thought I really wasn't going to loosen my grip on him. He told me that he hadn't yet gone to his Father."

"You are mad, woman," Philip said.

"It's truth. All of it."

The men gathered upstairs.

"You believe me, right?" Mary Magdalene asked Mary when they were alone.

"It's rather amazing."

Mary Magdalene grew quiet. "I finally saw him the way you do." She met eyes with Mary. "I really didn't want to let him go. I could have stayed in that garden hugging him with every breath he would give me."

Mary nodded.

"It was like when you told me about the day you anointed him. At that moment, he was the center of my whole world. Everything else circled around him. I would've done anything he asked."

At The Midday

"Saying, 'The Lord is risen indeed, and hath appeared to Simon.' "
-LUKE 24:34

Hours later

A small knock at the backdoor roused John and Andrew. They went to discover a group of brothers seeking them.

"Joseph! James! Judas! My sons!" Mary of Nazareth shouted. She ran to each and kissed their cheeks.

"Cleophas?" Aunt Mary called to her husband.

He embraced his wife. "I'm so glad to find you well. There has been much talk in the city."

"What are all of you doing here?" Mary of Nazareth asked.

"When we heard about the Crucifixion, Cleophas agreed to help us find you," Judas said.

"We had to make sure our mother was safe," Joseph added.

"Mother is perfectly safe with us," John protested.

"She is not your mother, she is ours," James argued.

"She is his mother as well," Mary added, without care for her place.

"Pardon?" Joseph asked.

"You weren't there." Mary's eyes filled with tears at the fresh memory. "You... weren't... there."

Silence fell over the arguing men.

"John was," she continued. "He sat with us under that hill and watched. Watched for hours as we saw him struggle for every breath. And with one of those precious breaths Jesus, himself, gave care of your mother to John. Him," Mary pointed to the young man. "Not you. Can't you give your dead brother that much honor to stop arguing? We care for her too. She means just as much to us. Jesus left her in John's care." She spun around and went into another room.

Mary Magdalene came in a few moments later. "Are you well?"

Mary nodded.

"I'd have thought you mad for speaking the way you did." She stroked Mary's unkempt hair.

"I just couldn't take their bickering any longer." Mary pulled her legs closer to her body. "Jesus has been gone only a few days and they are fighting about such petty things."

"You know he's not dead anymore."

Mary gave her friend a tired look. "I want to believe it. I really do. Regardless, Mother can take care of herself. She has been taking care of all of us and raised eight children mostly on her own."

"I had God's strength," Mary of Nazareth said, as she entered and went to sit beside the two women.

"Forgive me," Mary said with a duck of her head.

"You only speak truth." She rubbed Mary's arm. "There is nothing to forgive."

"Sisters," Aunt Mary entered the room.

Mary saw tears in her eyes.

"What is it?" Mary of Nazareth rose and went to her.

"We can't stay here anymore," Aunt Mary said over contained sobs. "Cleophas says it's not safe."

"Oh, sister," Mother said, pulling her into herself.

"I can't..." Aunt Mary wept. "Cleophas wants to go stay with friends in Emmaus. Seeing what they did to-"

"Mary," Cleophas called.

She looked up into the women's faces around her. "I'm sorry. We can't stay in Jerusalem anymore."

"Go in peace," Mary of Nazareth said to her sister.

"Why aren't we leaving for Galilee?" Mary

Magdalene asked, while gathered with the women in their small room.

Mary bent to hand her a bowl of lentils. "The men still aren't sure."

"Don't they believe us? The angel told us to go and we would meet Jesus in Galilee."

"They want to be cautious," she offered. "Caiaphas thinks the men moved the body. There is a high price on their heads. If we try to move such a large group of people, they are sure to find us. The men are simply trying to come up with a plan for all of us to get out of Jerusalem alive."

"But, the angel told us that Jesus would be waiting for us in Galilee. Surely, he would make sure we could arrive safely. He did just raise himself from the dead."

Mary sat beside her friend. "I know what you are saying and I agree with you. If Jesus is raised, then he has the power to protect us. The men are simply looking out for our safety."

"It's getting dark," Mary Magdalene said over a bite. "Maybe we could sneak out after the gates are closed. You said you know the streets well."

"I believe it best that we follow the men's lead and-"

"I know." She stuffed another bite in her mouth. When she swallowed, she added, "But it doesn't mean I have to like it."

Pounding startled the entire house.

"It's the Temple guards," Susanna cried. "They've found us."

"Quiet her," Andrew said to Mary.

Mary pulled her into a side room.

"The rest of you go as well," he called to the other women.

John and Andrew cautiously made their way to the door and unlocked it.

Peter stormed in, grabbing his chest. "I've seen him!"

"Peace," Andrew said, snatching his brother's arm. "Seen who?"

"Jesus!" His large chest heaved. "I'm telling you, it was him."

"Where?"

"I was in the city trying to gather information and see how much trouble was stirred. While I was on my way back here, there he was, he simply appeared-"

"He is risen!" a voice boomed through the open door.

Mary rushed out of the room to see Cleophas and Aunt Mary come in behind Peter.

Aunt Mary carried the brightest light in her face. Her eyes almost danced with joy. "We've seen him. He lives."

"Slow down," John said. "Seen who?"

"Jesus," Cleophas answered. "We were on the road and had made it almost to Emmaus when this man appeared with us."

"We didn't recognize him at first," Aunt Mary said.

"He spoke like a stranger," Cleophas

explained.

"We told him all about the events of the last few days," Aunt Mary added.

"Yes," Cleophas said. "Then he taught us as we walked. When we ate a meal together, he started at Moses and taught us everything concerning himself. When we saw him break the bread-"

"It all made sense," Aunt Mary said. "It was like lightning in my mind. It was just like you said, Mary." She turned to the younger woman. "He really is Messiah." She turned to Mary Magdalene. "And I'm sorry I didn't believe you. He was alive and well, just like you said."

"Come," Cleophas called to the group. "Let us share with you what he said."

As he finished repeating all that Jesus had told them, a bright light filled the room. It was so bright that Mary had to shield her eyes. The light so filled the room, that even the smallest shadow had to flee. When she blinked enough to see into the light, a man stood among them.

"Peace unto you," the voice proclaimed.

As her eyes adjusted even more, she could finally look upon his face. "Jesus," she whispered. "Jesus." Before she knew it, her face was on the dirt floor at his feet.

The group of them each bowed in turn and embraced Jesus for some time.

"Is it really you?" Simon asked.

Jesus lifted his sleeves to show his wrists and then lifted his garment to show his side.

Mary reached out and touched the open wounds. She knew exactly where they should be because she had seen them close up. She had watched the Roman soldiers rip the thick spikes out of his dead flesh. The holes were identical to the ones burned into her memory.

Jesus spoke again, "I'm giving you my peace. As my Father has sent me, so I send you." He took a deep breath and blew on them. "Receive the Holy Spirit."

Mary inhaled his sweet scent. She closed her eyes and felt a deep warmth fill her from the inside out. When she opened her eyes, Jesus was gone. She looked around and searched the rooms. "Where is he?"

"Did anyone see him leave?" Peter asked.

Everyone shook their heads and joined the search with Mary.

A knock came at the door.

Mary's heart jumped. She looked at Susanna, who was biting her bottom lip.

John exchanged a glance with Peter, who joined him in finding out who was on the other side.

When the door was open, a man slid in and quickly pushed it closed behind himself.

"Thomas!" James bar-Alpheus said.

"Keep quiet, man," Thomas said, rushing to cover James bar-Alpheus' mouth. "Do you know what is going on out in the streets. The whole city is unsettled."

"Thomas, we've seen him!" Mary shouted.

"What is that mad woman going on about?" he asked John.

"It's true," Peter said. "We've all seen the Lord. Jesus. He was just here."

"Jesus?" Thomas scoffed. "He's dead and buried."

"We saw him and touched him," Mary argued.

"If I don't see the nail holes with my own eyes or put my finger into his side for myself," he said, thrusting his hand to his ribs. "I will not believe it's true."

"If you had been here, you would have," Mary said and left the room.

A few days later, Mary was heading back to the borrowed house from Bethany with two shoulder bags full of food. Roman anger had cooled slightly, but it was still dangerous for the group of them to be out for too long. The women had offered a solution to buying the things they need. Each woman would be sent into a nearby town, bought what she could with their limited resources, and return as secretly as she could.

She wandered into a large open field in search of any fruit trees or vines she could pick from to add a special treat to her collection. The land was sparse, but she did see a large tree off in the distance.

Squinting against the sun, Mary tried to see it more clearly because something seemed off about what her eyes were trying to show her. She walked closer to the barren tree and when she came about a stone's throw away, she covered her mouth, but it was too late. A loud scream had already escaped and she found herself smothering the noise.

Trying to close her eyes, Mary spun around and desperately tried to remove the image from her mind's eye. It was a useless attempt. The face of Judas Iscariot's wide, black eyes stared back at her. She opened her eyes again and looked over her shoulder. The same dark eyes stared down at her. Lifeless.

His bloated body hung from one of the tree limbs and it spun in the wind. She turned to face the wicked display. Tracing his face with her eyes, she came to his neck and met the end of a rope tied there.

When the wind shifted, it forced her to cover her mouth with her headscarf. The stench that came off his dead body as it baked in the sun was overwhelming.

She stepped back slowly. As she did, she heard the branch start to give way. The cracking of wood grew louder as the branch snapped at the point where the rope was tied. Her eyes followed his body as it hit the ground and split open.

Mary shook her head in horror as the man's insides spilled out on the thirsty ground. The liquid that poured out of the opening turned the soil dark. The smell filled her already covered nose.

She took a few more steps backward to try to get away, but her feet would not break into a run even as she pleaded for them to do so. Just then, she heard a loud howl that caused her attention to be drawn to the north. Several wild dogs were heading her way from over the horizon.

She was finally able to turn her body around and run from the gruesome scene. She regretted looking back because, as she did, she saw the dogs reach the feast laid out before them. The first one who had reached the meal was raising his head out of the bloody mess to signal the others as she turned back to face the direction of her path.

Mary didn't stop running when she made it to the gates of Jerusalem. She didn't care who noticed her. They would have to catch her if they wanted to question her. She wanted to put as much distance between herself and that awful sight that plagued her.

She found the borrowed house in Jerusalem and burst through the door. Her screams were cut short by panting from the run.

"Calm down." John came over to her and shook her shoulders.

"What has gotten into that girl?" Mary of Nazareth asked from across the large room.

Mary looked into John's brown eyes and focused on them to calm herself. Then she broke out into tears in his arms. "The body...the body...dogs." She pointed a shaking finger toward the door.

"Breathe, Mary. Breathe," John said slowly.

She took a few deep breaths to calm her racing heart and catch her breath.

"Now," he said. "What happened?"

Closing her eyes and wetting her lips, Mary said, "I went for a walk after I saw my family. I was trying to clear my head before coming back here with the food. There was this field and a tree." She took another deep breath and tried to remind herself to stay calm. "Judas Iscariot. He hung from a tree in the middle of this field, but while I was looking at him, the branch snapped and his body hit the ground. It hit so hard that it opened up and everything came out. These dogs came and started eating his in-"

John held up a hand. "That's enough."

Breathing deep, Mary looked around at the shocked faces that now surrounded her.

"Judas Iscariot?" Andrew asked. "You're sure?"

Mary nodded.

"Come over here, dear." Mary of Nazareth grabbed her shoulders and led her across the room. "Sit down and take it easy."

Mary let the words of the men gathered in the courtyard wash over her in a collection of noise while her mind closed under the pressure of all the recent events.

"We need to go make sure," she heard Andrew say.

"It's too dangerous," John replied.

"What if she was mistaken?" Andrew asked. "We need to know for sure."

"Agreed," Simon said. "Matthew and I can go. We'll be able to make it out and back before the gates close."

John nodded. "Take extreme precaution."

When they had left and Mary had let her thoughts come back to the present, she noticed Mary of Nazareth laying out the platters for the evening meal. "Smells good."

She glanced down at her. "Thank you."

Mary sighed.

"Don't worry, sweet girl," she said. "That man was not worth the rope he hung himself with."

"You think he did it to himself?"

Without stopping, she nodded.

"He betrayed Jesus," Mary said without thinking.

Mary of Nazareth stopped and closed her eyes. "Yes, he did."

"Oh, Mother, I'm sorry. I-"

"It's alright." She shook her head. "We each make our own choices in life."

Mary went back to helping her spread out the food for the band of men.

Night began to fall when Matthew and Simon returned.

As the group ate, the two recounted their

findings.

"It's true," Simon said. "We found him just as Mary said."

"We went to the Temple," Matthew interjected. "Asked around to find out any more information. Seems, he had gone to the priests to return the silver they offered him."

"Silver?" John asked.

"Thirty pieces was the agreed offer they made to Judas Iscariot for his betrayal that night."

"That snake," Andrew said. "John told us he was taking money from the treasurer's bag, but we didn't believe him. If I had a few moments with him, I would have-"

"But he tried to give it back," Matthew continued. "When he found out that Pilate agreed to crucify Jesus. He went to the priest and gave them the silver back."

"We should have trusted you with the bag, Matthew," Simon said. "You were a tax collector for mercy's sake. Why Jesus ever trusted such a despicable person is beyond me."

"It doesn't matter much now," Matthew offered.

"So why was he found hung?" James asked.

"It took a few inquiries," Matthew said. "But we found out that they denied his request to rescind the betrayal."

"Rumor has it they are using the silver to buy the land his blood has stained," Simon added.

Mary had enough of the talk. She made her

way to one of the side rooms and laid on the dirt floor.

Several days later, the group of men and women were still taking refuge in the borrowed house. The owner had informed them that they could stay as long as they wished. He supplied them with food from the market and from his supply of animals and storage. Though it was many more mouths than he was accustomed to feeding, every day there seemed to be enough.

Friends in the city also kept word coming if anyone was getting close to discovering their hideout. Plus, they were doing an excellent job of spreading false rumors to keep the High Priests and Romans running down false leads.

Mary stood, leaning against one of the support beams in the open courtyard of the house. The joy and peace that Jesus had left her with were still at the surface of her heart. She couldn't keep the grin off her face, but she missed him. She missed him terribly. She stared at the place Jesus' feet had been the week before. All of a sudden, a pair of feet filled the empty space. Following the legs up, she met his face.

"Greetings, Mary," he said with a smile.

She hurried to embrace him.

Others came into the courtyard and exchanged

greetings.

Thomas stepped in from a side room.

Jesus walked over to him. "Thomas," he said softly. "Reach your finger here." He rolled up his sleeve to reveal one of the large holes in his wrist. "Or here." He lifted his tunic and pointed to the slice in his side. "Stop doubting and believe."

Thomas fell at his feet. "My Lord and my God." He wrapped his arms around Jesus' legs and buried his face in his tunic.

Jesus patted his head. "You believe because you have seen me. Blessed are those who haven't seen and still believe."

"Will you stay?" Mary pleaded through blurry eyes.

Jesus nodded. "For a little while."

The group sat together over a meal in the upper room before Jesus disappeared again.

Two weeks later found the large group sitting in the courtyard of the borrowed home.

"I can't take this anymore," Peter said. He kicked the dirt. "I've got to get out of here."

"Peace, brother," Andrew said.

"I will not." He stormed up the steps to the upper room.

John shrugged to Andrew.

When Peter returned, he had his outer cloak

on and a bag in his hand. "I'm going home to Galilee. Anyone who wants to come with me is welcome."

"Wait." Andrew stepped in front of his brother.

"No, not this time."

"I know you're upset about what happened at Caiaphas' house."

"This isn't about that. He said he would be back or send us a sign, but nothing has happened."

"We just need to have faith," Andrew said.

"I'm tired, brother. I'm tired of waiting. I'm tired of hiding in this house." He waved around the room.

"But Rome-"

"I don't care anymore." He put the bag strap over his shoulder. "I'm going home."

"And just what are you going to do?" Andrew asked.

"I'm going fishing," Peter said with a slam of the front door.

"We have to go after him," Bartholomew said.

"I agree," Thomas said. "We need to bring him back."

"I don't think he'll listen," John said.

"Then what are we going to do?" Thaddeus asked.

"I guess we're going home," Andrew said.

The men began to gather supplies for the journey.

"John, you can't go," Mary begged.

"We told you women that any of you are more than welcome to come with us."

"We need to stay here where it's safe."

"It's growing less safe with each passing day." He shoved a loaf of bread into a bag.

"I've talked it over with the other women." She paused. "We've decided to stay here. Mother thinks Jesus will be back any day."

John stopped packing his bag, but didn't look up.

"You don't think he is coming back."

"I just don't know anymore." He put a handful of dried fruit in the bag. "At least we can go back to doing something we know."

When the door shut behind the group of men, Mary looked around to find the eyes of Simon, Philip, James bar-Alpheus, and Matthew. They had decided to stay in Jerusalem. The men exchanged glances with each other as well.

"Let's go pray that they will arrive safely at their destination," Matthew said and headed up the steps.

Mary knelt and whispered a few prayers of her own.

At The City

"Jesus saith unto them, 'Come and dine.' And none of the disciples durst ask him, 'Who art thou?' knowing that it was the Lord."
-JOHN 21:12

Three Weeks Later

Mary swept the sand out of the back door of the borrowed house. She had spent so much time in it the past month, that it was beginning to feel like home. A rare day would find her traveling to Bethany with Mary Magdalene or Mary of Nazareth to visit Lazarus and Martha. Most days found the women and a handful of the men in the house. They fasted, prayed, and ate together.

The city had calmed somewhat, but the men were always uneasy about leaving the safety of the house. They only allowed the women to leave to buy food or supplies under duress and pleas for a quick return. The men couldn't travel as easily as the women, who were less recognizable.

Though it was a life of hiding, Mary found more contentment with her friends than any she had encountered before. Love and peace reigned in their hearts and she had never felt the heights of closeness with God more than when she gathered with the others. Every time they prayed, every time they spoke of one of Jesus' teachings, it was like he was right there with them again.

Satisfied with her chore, Mary went into the kitchen to find Joanna and Susanna chopping vegetables for a stew.

"It smells wonderful," Mary said, sniffing the air.

"We've only just begun," Joanna said.

"Anything I can help with?" Mary offered.

Susanna handed her the knife in her hand. "Here. I'm going to fetch some clean water." She picked up the empty water jug and lifted it to her hip.

"Hurry back," Matthew commanded.

She nodded and opened the door.

Men began to pour in the opening, pressing the small woman back inside, and then shut the door.

"You'll never guess what happened to us!" John shouted.

"Boys!" Mary of Nazareth called from across the courtyard. "Are you well?" she asked while kissing each man's cheek.

"We are well, Mother," John said, holding the older woman at arm's length. "You look well."

"I am. No thanks to you." She swatted at him with the rag in her hand. "You were supposed to be taking care of this old woman and you go running off with the others," she kidded.

"Forgive me, but we have seen him."

Her eyes widened. "Jesus?"

John nodded vigorously.

"Sit," she commanded. "Sit down here and tell me everything."

"You must be hungry," Joanna offered. "I'll serve you some food."

"Speak," Mary of Nazareth said, sitting among the men.

Mary stood behind them, listening to their tale on the Sea of Galilee.

"We had been out one night, without catching a single thing," James started.

"We should have guessed that was going to happen to a couple of rusty fishermen," Andrew added, with an elbow jab to Peter.

Peter kept his glance to the ground between his feet.

"The sun was just beginning to rise when we decided to head for shore," James continued.

"There was someone standing on the shore," Thaddeus said. "He called out to us, asking if we had caught any fish."

"Of course, we hadn't," Thomas said, taking some dried fruit off the platter Joanna had placed in the middle of them.

"I'm sure he knew that," James said.

"That's how I knew it was Jesus," John said. "I told Peter it was him."

"As soon as he did," Bartholomew joked. "Peter here puts his coat on and jumps into the water."

"Yes," James said. "Straight into the water and swam to shore."

"Leaving the rest of us to row the boat back," Thomas added.

"We could have used his help too," Andrew said.

"Why?" Mary asked.

"We were bringing in the net," John answered. "It was full of fish!"

"I thought you said you didn't catch anything," Mary said.

"We didn't," John went on. "Until Jesus showed up. Before I told Peter who it was, Jesus told us to cast our net on the other side of the boat. When I saw the net full of fish, it only confirmed to me that it was him."

"I thought the net was going to break," Thomas said.

"Me too," Thaddeus added.

"It reminded me of when Jesus called us to follow him the first time," John said. "It was like he was calling us all over again. My heart burned within me the closer we got to shore."

"When we did get to shore," James said. "He was there waiting for us."

"With a fire and breakfast cooking like he had been waiting for us all night," Andrew said. He looked over at his brother. "Tell them, Peter. You made it to shore first."

For the first time since they sat, Peter looked up at the group. Mary could see something clouding his thoughts. His face was a mix of emotions that she couldn't clearly pick out. He took a breath and said, "I had just crawled up the sandy shore. My entire body was soaked. When I looked up, I saw him sitting by a fire staring at me.

"A gust of wind kicked up and the smoke from the fire slapped me across the face. The smell of burning coals invaded my nostrils. It produced flashes of memories in my mind. The last time I was over a coal fire was that night in Caiaphas' courtyard. The night I-" He glanced at Mary of Nazareth. "The night I betrayed him," his voice cracked and he cleared his throat. "The smell drove my face into the wet sand around me. Tears flowed freely and mixed with the water pooling around me dripping from my clothes.

"I had traded the past three years of some of the sweetest fellowship I had ever known for fear of being hung beside him. I had not only denied following him, but I had also denied even knowing him. Can you ever forgive me, Mother?" he asked.

She nodded carefully. "Of course."

He swallowed hard and continued, "I dug my hands into the sand and threw fists full over myself. I wept in deep mourning. That's when I heard his voice."

"Jesus?" Mary asked.

"Yes. He was calling to the men behind me.

Telling them to bring some of their fish to add to the meal. I looked over my shoulder to see them dragging the net onto the shore. It was so full."

"And heavy," Thomas added.

"Shh," Andrew said.

"I helped them count the catch," Peter said.

"153," Andrew said.

"153," Peter repeated. "Enough to fetch a good price. I glanced over at Jesus, who was flipping some flatbread over the fire. The smell of the bread brought back the feast of that same night. With his arms wide open, he invited us to eat with him."

"And we feasted," Thaddeus said, rubbing his stomach.

"He passed around the warm bread and baked fish, just like that night. He was serving us all over again," Peter went on. "We all sat there quietly waiting for him to start teaching."

"We were so eager to hear from his lips," James said.

"Lips that should have been motionless and cold in the grave," John added.

"I just sat there staring into the dancing flames," Peter said. "I barely ate my portion. Not for the anticipation of a lesson or even tired from my swim. It was guilt that invaded my soul. I was reliving the events of that fateful night over and over again, trying to will them to be different. That's when he spoke." He met his brother's eyes. "He called my name and asked if I loved him more than any of the things that surrounded us."

"What did you say?" Mary asked.

"Of course I did and I told him so. I had given them all up once before. I had left my family and everything I knew to follow him. I would do it again." He rubbed his dark beard. "He told me to feed his lambs."

"His lambs?" Mary wondered.

"I didn't get it either. Then he asked me again if I loved him more than anything. I, again, said yes. He told me to feed his sheep. Again, a third time, he asked if I loved him." Peter paused and scratched his head. "I had answered his question repeatedly. I was pretty frustrated at that point, but told him that I knew he already knew everything and knew that I loved him. He sat there calmly and asked for me to feed his sheep."

"That's when he asked you to go with him away from us," Andrew said.

Peter nodded.

"What did you speak about?" Thaddeus asked.

Peter looked down. "He told me how I was going to die."

A gasp escaped Mary's mouth.

For several moments, silence hung as heavy as a dark night.

Peter continued without looking anyone in the eye, "He told me that while I am young, I will go wherever I want to go and be able to support myself, but one day will come when that will change. When I am old, I will stretch out my hand

and someone else will support me and lead me where I don't want to go.

"I didn't understand at first, but on the journey here the more I thought about it the more it had to be about my death. That, somehow, I will be physically led to my own death."

Thoughts swirled in Mary. "You said Jesus asked you three times if you loved him?"

Peter met her eyes and nodded. "The same question, three times, yes."

"How many times did you deny him?"

"Mary!" John scolded. "I spoke that to you in private."

Peter rose. "Let her speak." He took a step closer to her. "Speak on."

"How many times did you deny Jesus?"

"Three."

"And he asked the same question three times?"

Peter took another step. "What are you getting at?"

"I don't think it was for naught. I think he was trying to show you something."

"What?"

"That you do love him. Even though you denied him three times, you declared your love and willingness to obey three times. He was, in a sense, restoring you."

Peter cupped his chin and rubbed it several times as he studied the floor. "It does make sense."

"And what of the sheep?" Thomas asked.

"I had already figured that out," Peter said.

"His people," Mary said. "He told us he was the Good Shepherd and his sheep would follow his voice. He was reinstating Peter as a leader."

Peter nodded.

Later that evening, Jesus appeared to them again.

"Where have you been?" Mary asked, not wishing to let him go. Each time he appeared, she knew he would have to eventually leave. "Please stay," she pleaded with her eyes and her heart.

He cupped her face in his hand. "One day, nothing will separate us."

She smiled and rubbed her cheek into his palm.

The group gathered around him. "It's time."

Without another word, they followed him out of the house. They walked in silence as he led them out of the city and toward the east.

Mary knew the path, it led home. She had walked it more times than she could count. It had been a few days since she saw her brother and sister. She wondered if Jesus was planning on a visit with them.

When they reached the far side of the Mount of Olives, Jesus stopped. He gathered them around himself. Reaching out his hands, he prayed over them and blessed them. "I need you to stay here in Jerusalem for a little longer," Jesus explained.

"Stay here?" Simon asked.

"Yes. Wait for the promise of the Father. The One I told you about before. He will remind you of me. John baptized with water, but you will be baptized with the Holy Spirit soon."

"Lord," James said. "When will you restore your kingdom in Israel?"

"You can't know the time or season, only the Father knows. When the Holy Spirit comes upon you, you will receive power." Jesus looked over all of them. "You will be my witnesses in Jerusalem, in all of Judea, in Samaria, and even to the ends of the world."

Out of nowhere, Jesus' feet slowly left the ground.

Mary's eyes followed him up. Soon he was above their heads.

Mary's heart leapt within her. She wanted to reach up and pull his foot back down. She saw the nail hole and began to weep. *Please don't leave.* As she watched, he was lifted further until he went past the clouds and beyond her vision. She stood there looking up and waiting. Hoping that at any moment, he would come back down.

"Men of Galilee," a voice called.

It brought Mary's attention back to the ground.

A man dressed all in white stood among them. He was beautiful. He looked like the man she saw in the garden. A light was beaming from within him and shone all around him. She had never seen an angel this close.

"Why do you stand here gazing up into the sky?" he asked.

Mary watched the men glance to each other and then back at the man in white. They saw him too and couldn't place him. She saw Mary of Nazareth and Mary Magdalene nod to each other. It seemed as if they knew the man. She wondered if he was the angel who spoke to them at the tomb.

"Jesus, the same one who was taken up from you into heaven, he will come back the same way."

Mary looked back up into the sky. She squinted, hoping to catch a glimpse of Jesus.

At The Feast Of Weeks

"And there appeared unto them cloven tongues like as of fire, and it sat upon each of them."
-ACTS 2:3

40 Days After Passover

Mary gathered with Jesus' followers in the Temple just after sunrise. Peter had brought them together many times to the Temple in the past weeks. They had spent wonderful times in prayer together.

Today a large group gathered with them. They had been faithful to spread Jesus' message and tell others. Many believed and joined them in their sessions at the Temple.

"Brothers." Peter stood in the middle of them. "We know that all the events happened to fulfill what the prophets spoke concerning Judas Iscariot. He was one of us."

Andrew huffed.

"The land on which he hung himself is now separated and called the field of blood. It has happened just as it was written." He took a breath.

"And now we need to move forward with what our Lord has told us. We need to choose another to take Judas Iscariot's place." He waved two men forward. "These are Joseph Justus and Matthias."

The two stood in the center with Peter.

"Let us pray that God will show us which of these honorable men will be counted among us."

Mary whispered prayers along with the others as they watched the lots be cast before the two men. The lot fell to Matthias.

"Matthias, you will take on the ministry that was given to Judas Iscariot," Peter said. "You will go in his place."

Matthias bowed deeply.

The large group joined them back at the borrowed house for a meal.

Mary stirred the cooking fire as Peter led the men in prayer.

Suddenly, a roar filled the room.

Mary covered her ears.

The flames of the fire danced for a moment in the rushing wind and then died. Its light was rapidly replaced with bright flames that hung over them.

"They look like tongues," John said, pointing up at them.

Mary was glad she wasn't the only one seeing the unbelievable sight.

One came close to her and rested on her head.

Fear rose inside her for a brief moment before it was overtaken with peace. She knew this peace.

It was the same feeling that filled her when Jesus breathed on her. The Holy Spirit filled her from the inside out.

When she opened her mouth to speak, she heard a strange sound. Her tongue felt different in her mouth and her words were unfamiliar to her own ears.

The rest of them rushed from one to another speaking strange words.

Some of the men hurried outside and began to speak to people who passed by. It wasn't long before the group attracted a mass of people.

"They are drunk with much wine," a man called from the crowd.

"Can you not hear?" someone else yelled at him. "They are speaking my native language."

"And mine!" another shouted.

"Aren't they Galileans?" the first asked. "How can they know all these languages?"

Peter stood up on a step to speak, "Men of Judea, we are not drunk. It is only the third hour of the morning." He waved his hands to demand their complete attention. "This was spoken to you by the prophet Joel. He said, 'And it shall come to pass in the last days, says God, I will pour out my Spirit upon all flesh. Your sons and daughters will prophesy. Your young men will see visions and your old men will dream dreams. On servants and handmaidens, will I pour out my Spirit and they will prophesy as well? I will show wonders in the sky above and on the earth below. Blood, fire, and vapors of smoke. The sun will be turned to darkness and the moon to blood. Before the great and notable day of the Lord's coming. It will come to pass that whosoever will call on the name of the Lord will be saved.' Men of Israel, listen to these words.

"Jesus of Nazareth is a man approved of God with miracles, wonders, and signs. You knew him. The same man, who was delivered by the determinate counsel and foreknowledge of God, you took and crucified."

Murmurs spread through the crowd.

"God raised him up, having released the pains of death on him because it was not possible for him to stay dead. David spoke of him saying, 'I foresaw the Lord before my face for he is on my right hand that I should not be moved. Therefore, did my heart rejoice and my tongue was glad. Moreover, my flesh will also rest in hope because you will not leave my soul in the realm of the dead. Neither will you stand by and let the Holy One see corruption. You have made known to me the ways of life. You will make me full of joy with your presence.' Brothers, let me speak freely.

"Our patriarch David is both dead and buried. You know where his sepulcher is even today. So, being a prophet, he knew that God had sworn an oath to him and that the fruit of his loins would rise up and sit on his throne. He was speaking about Jesus. He spoke of the resurrection of Jesus, that his soul would not be left in the land of the dead nor his flesh see corruption. God raised Jesus from the dead. We are all witnesses." Peter waved around to the group Mary was standing in. "We have seen his undead flesh and touch the nail holes. He has eaten with us and showed himself to us. God raised Jesus to his right hand and has given us the promise of the Holy Spirit. It is that Holy Spirit that you have experienced with us today.

"David did not ascend into the heavens, but Jesus did. David also said that God would tell Jesus to sit on His right hand and make His foes a footstool. So, let all the house of Israel know for sure, God has made this same Jesus, whom you crucified, both Lord and Messiah."

Mary watched the words of Peter run across the people's faces.

"What shall we do?" one asked.

Peter smiled wide. "Repent. Repent and be baptized in the name of Jesus for the cancellation of your debt of sin. Then you will receive the gift of the Holy Spirit. This promise was made unto you, your children, and all those who are far away. Any whom the Lord our God will call."

Mary had the great pleasure of walking with many men and women who followed Peter and the others down to the river to baptize those who wanted their sins forgiven by Jesus.

At The Meeting

"It seemed good to me also, having had perfect understanding of all things from the very first, to write unto thee..."
-LUKE 1:3

A.D. 60, Bethany

Mary opened her front door to find a familiar face on the other side. "Doctor Luke," she said. "Please come in."

"I wasn't sure if you would recognize me." He stepped inside. "It has been some time."

"I could never forget your face. It was your advice that kept our brother less ill for many decades."

"Mary, who is at the front door?" Martha came in the back door from outside. When she recognized the man standing with Mary, she ran to him. "Doctor Luke," she said with a kiss on his cheek. "What a wonderful surprise."

"Always good to see you," he said. "Where is your brother?"

"Here," Lazarus called from across the

courtyard.

"You look as healthy as a favored sheep."

"He's been that way since Jesus raised him from the dead," Martha said.

"I heard that tale."

"Shame, though. I thought I was finally going to get some peace around here," Martha teased.

"Oh, woman!" Lazarus huffed and shooed her away.

"Can I offer you some dried fruit?" Martha said on her way to the kitchen. "I have some fresh bread cooking as well."

"Please," Luke said, placing his bag on the floor. "It's been a long journey."

"As good as it is to see you," Lazarus said. "We didn't call for a doctor. What brings you to Bethany?"

"In a way, Mary does."

"Me?"

"Yes, I've been traveling for some time now gathering eyewitness accounts of the things Jesus did and taught." He took a few pieces of dried fruit from the tray Martha placed in front of him. "I wish to write an account, if you will, of him."

"Jesus?" Mary asked.

"I've been commissioned by a friend, Theophilus, to gather recorded facts and testimonies to the things Jesus did while he was here."

"Sounds like a big task," Martha said.

"I'm most interested in events that brought

you to your place of understanding, Mary."

"Why me? Many others have greater stories to tell than me."

"I've spoken to a great number of them. You Jewish people share your history among yourselves quite well and have come to much understanding of Jesus as Messiah." He took a sip of water to clear his dry throat from traveling the dusty roads. "I'm interested in sharing Jesus with a Gentile audience to show he was much more than just a man from God, but more of a God-man."

"And so, you came to hear from Mary?" Lazarus asked.

"I visited Mary of Nazareth, Jesus' mother before she died and I spoke to your friend, Mary Magdalene as well. She had many stories to tell and suggested I come speak with you. She told me about the day you anointed Jesus."

Mary smiled as she recalled that day. "Oh, yes. I remember it well."

"Knowing you would do me the honor of receiving me as a friend, I was hoping you could give me a little more detail about that day and why you did what you did."

"I don't know if I feel comfortable sharing the details with you. We are under a time of great persecution."

"If the Romans found out that Mary was one of his followers," Lazarus warned. "She could be in great danger."

"Not to mention, if the Jews have testimony of her deeds," Martha added. "She could be brought before the High Council."

"I understand your concern," Luke reassured them. "My goal here today is not to cause grief and trouble for you. Simply to tell your story."

Mary sat quietly for a few moments.

"I'm not revealing many others' identities. I can tell your story without naming you." He reached out and patted the top of her hand. "I'm here for the facts."

Mary nodded. "That will be acceptable."

Luke dug through his bag for a writing stylus, inkwell, and papyrus. "Ready when you are."

She took a deep breath and brought her thoughts back to the days long ago. "I knew Jesus when we were children. He was a plain enough boy who grew up working with his father. His parents were not well off and he had several brothers and sisters. They would travel to Jerusalem for festivals and we would get to see them a few times a year.

"I always thought Jesus a bit odd. Actually," She thought for a few moments. "It was more than that. I held hatred in my heart against him for a very long time. I placed all of my problems squarely on his shoulders. Hidden under the guise that I believed him the root cause of our people's problems, of course. When, in fact, I blamed him for my own mess of a life. You see, so many miraculous things happened around his birth, that those in power sought to kill him."

"His mother told me some of the stories," Luke said. "Fascinating tales for a doctor." He smiled.

"Yes. Did she also tell you that while they fled to safety in Egypt, our region was ravaged by blood-hungry Roman soldiers? They killed so many babies, looking for Jesus. Our people paid the price for decades. My family lived with the consequences of that night." She looked at her brother and sister. "When you came to see us that first time, we told you that our mother had a difficult time while carrying Lazarus and he was sick from the beginning."

"I remember."

"She was under so much stress to produce a male child, as was every married woman. Many women were so heartbroken and in mourning after that night. It was awful. They lamented for years. They shared in each other's grief. I blamed Jesus for all of it. Of course, I was young and filled with hate."

"What changed?"

"When Jesus became a traveling teacher, he would often come back here to Bethany. We became sort of a safe place for him and his followers. A second home for them since they were so very far from their own homes and families. I got to spend much time with them.

"One day, I was listening to Jesus teach in the Temple. The Pharisees brought in a woman they claimed to have caught in the act of adultery."

"How could that happen?"

"It was common practice for them to set traps," Lazarus added. "They loved to find people breaking the laws."

"Yes. This poor woman was dragged, half-naked, into the crowded courtyard and tossed at Jesus' feet like a stray dog."

"What did he do?"

"Nothing. At first. He started writing in the sand without saying anything or even acknowledging any of them. After the Pharisees repeatedly questioned him about his position on stoning her-"

"Stoning her?"

"It is the punishment for such a crime."

"I see."

"Jesus finally looked up and told them that whichever one of them was without sin could throw the first stone at her. They were ready too. Each of them had already picked out their weapon and brought it with them." Mary grinned. "Then they just dropped them and walked away."

"They realized they had sinned also."

Mary nodded. "The best part. Jesus looked right into the woman's eyes. I mean, got down to her level and looked her right in the eyes. He asked her where her accusers were. She looked around to find none of them. He told her that he didn't accuse her either and that she was free to leave. He forgave her."

"Just like that?"

"Just like that. He didn't ask her any questions about her crime, neither did he condemn her for it. Obviously, he knew she was guilty. She never denied it either. He just forgave her and sent her on her way. It was that day that I thought about the hatred in my heart. I had been listening to him teach and had been a witness to many of his miracles. Yet, I still held this deep hate in my heart. He taught us that if you hate your brother, then it is just as bad as if you had murdered him with your own two hands. The pieces of his life were falling too well into place, lining up with what we had been taught to look for in our Messiah. How could I go on hating Messiah? How could I kill him in my heart?"

"That's when you decided to anoint him."

She nodded. "He kept speaking of his coming death. I wanted to show my love for him and also show him that I believed in what he was saying. So many of his followers didn't want to hear about his death. They only wanted to hear about his victory and how they could share in it. I wanted to show him that I wanted to share in his sacrifice. One of his disciples, Judas Iscariot-"

"The one who betrayed him."

"Yes. His father invited Jesus to his home. He was a Pharisee who had recovered from a season of leprosy. They lived here in Bethany and while Jesus was visiting us, Simon wanted to show off to Jesus. The men went to supper that night while the women stayed at my house.

"My father was a spice trader and kept many oils in our private storage. I knew we had a bottle of Spikenard because it was our mother's favorite. I took it and went to Simon's house. I was so overwhelmed with this burden to anoint him. It was like something was pulling me toward him that night.

"I still can't believe she did what she did," Lazarus added. "It was a great dishonor to come into a feast of men uninvited, as an unaccompanied woman, and then to uncover her hair in front of all those men. I had to hide my rage in front of the rest of them."

"Not to mention I was not exactly the cleanest of women," Mary said.

"I don't understand."

"Not long after my father died, I became a harlot. It was not something I was proud of, but I did what I had to in order to provide for my siblings. Actually," she considered. "It was just after we met for the first time."

"Really?"

"Yes. When you told Martha and me what it would take to keep our brother well, I knew it would cost a lot of money."

"I didn't mean-"

She held up her hand to stop him. "You did nothing wrong. It was my own choice. I'm grateful for your wisdom. If not for you, our brother would have died long ago."

"When did you stop?"

"I decided not to give myself over for money the same day I saw Jesus forgive that woman. It wasn't something I talked about with anyone. Thankfully, I had saved enough of my earnings to help sustain my family. I bought back my mother's vineyard and began working it. Later, when Jesus raised Lazarus from the dead, Lazarus was able to work and earn a wage. It wasn't until the dinner in which I anointed him that Jesus forgave my sins. Jesus didn't care about my old profession. Like the woman caught in adultery, he simply forgave me and sent me on my way."

"How could he forgive sins?"

"Messiah can. He is God. God alone can forgive sins."

"Mary Magdalene said you were anointing his body for burial."

"I had prepared bodies for burial a few times before and seen it done on numerous occasions. He kept urgently speaking of his upcoming death. With everything in me, I knew he spoke truth. Why would he be lying about that? He never lied about anything before. Every one of his words happened precisely as he said.

"I walked into that dinner preparing to say thank you. I walked out being forgiven of my sins. Jesus was the one who talked about his burial, even that very night. He told the men who were seething with rage to leave me alone. I imagine without his command of protection, they would have hunted me down and stoned me."

"I know it crossed my mind," Lazarus said.

"He told them I had done it in preparation for his burial and that my story would live on as a testimony of what I had done."

"The act of anointing him?"

"Not just the anointing. I had believed him. I had taken him at his word and believed him with everything in me." She took a breath. "That's what he was looking for in his followers. That we would trust him even when things didn't make sense."

"Faith?"

"Exactly. I didn't understand what he was saying about why he had to die, but I had faith that what he said was going to happen would happen."

"I see."

"And it did. Everything he said happened just as he said it was going to."

Luke fervently scribbled on the parchment in his hand.

"You have much medical training, yes?" Mary asked.

"Yes," he said, looking up from his writing.

"Can I ask you a medical question?"

"I'll do my best to answer."

"The night of Jesus' trial, he was praying in the garden. It was a very dark night, but I saw something on his forehead."

"Blood," he said with a downcast look. "When I spoke to some of the men who were there that night, they described it to me."

"He had not been injured. It was before they came for him."

"It can happen. It's rare, but it has been documented. They call it Hematohidrosis. You see, if a person is under a great deal of stress, the body reacts in several ways. One of them is that the capillaries in the forehead can burst and mix with sweat."

"You think that's what happened?" Mary asked.

"From the men's testimony, yes. I'd say that's exactly what happened."

"Why do you think he died so quickly on the cross?" Mary asked.

"Crucifixion is one of the most torturous ways a person can die. The Romans certainly have studied how to kill their prisoners slowly. As a man is nailed into place, they give his legs just enough room to press upward. This allows the lungs to open for a breath or two.

"Then the muscles in the arms and legs give way under the strain of having to hold up one's weight for hours. In doing so, the lungs are closed and the person begins to gasp for air. The process is repeated until the man can no longer lift himself up and ultimately succumbs to suffocation.

"In Jesus' case, since your testimony and others were that he was dead when they came to break his leg bones, his process was probably accelerated by the fact he had endured the scourging beforehand. Add in the blood loss, pain, mental stress, and back muscles being torn to shreds, it surprises me that he lasted as long as he did on the cross."

"And the spear?" Mary asked. "When the soldier stuck his spear into Jesus' side, the liquid that came out was more than blood. It was watery."

"Mary Magdalene spoke of that too. I believe, due also to the scourging that his body was in a state of shock. When the body undergoes such a tremendous amount of physical pain and beating, it tries to help itself. The heart beats rapidly trying to pump blood to the rest of the body, the person often faints, they might develop an extreme thirst and even loss of kidney function. The amount of time from his scourging until the spear pierced his side was several hours, correct?"

Mary nodded.

"With a sustained rapid heartbeat for that long, fluid often builds up in the sack around the heart. The spear could have punctured this and the resulting blood and fluid came out together." Luke sighed to himself. "It just goes to prove what an incredible amount of stress he was under."

"Yes, it was," Mary said.

Luke made notations on his parchment.

"Will you stay long in our region?" Lazarus asked.

"No. My traveling companions want to set out on another journey," Luke said. "I have a few more questions and then I have to get back to them before they head out."

"Why do they take you along?" Lazarus asked. "Wouldn't you do more good staying in one place?"

"No," Luke answered. "I travel with a man who caught a terrible eye disease in Galatia many years ago. Before he arrived there, he had been stoned almost to the point of death and it weakened his body. The church aided him as best they could, but he is nearly entirely blind.

"When I met him in Troas on his second journey, I agreed to continue with him as a personal medical aid. I've been able to help him minister to other believers and bring others into the fold. I also help the people in each city we visit. I believe it is what God has called me to do."

"Where are you heading now?" Mary asked.

"Rome. He feels led of God to go there. Even if…"

"If what?"

Luke looked up at her. "Even if it means certain death for him."

"Then why go?" Lazarus asked.

"He is to testify before Caesar himself. He's going to testify of Jesus to the most powerful man in our world. Who would pass up that chance?"

At The Cave

*"But God will redeem my soul from the power of
the grave: for he shall receive me."*
-PSALM 49:15

A.D. 66, Bethany

Mary stood at the mouth of the cave cut into the mountain as the two large men carried the body of her brother into the darkness. Tears slid down her cheeks as she watched them lay his body in one of the hollowed-out shelves of the wall. Other shelves held her father, mother, and sister. Now, she laid her brother with the rest of their family.

When they were done, the men rolled the boulder in front of the opening, then they left her alone. She walked up and placed her hand gently on the cold stone. Bending her forehead down onto the massive boulder, Mary tightly closed her eyes and thought about her family.

Every one of them was gone. Her parents when they were young, Martha due to an illness that prayer could not take away, and now Lazarus. His death had been at the hands of Florus' troops who stormed Jerusalem to calm the uproar against him. The Roman treasury officer had taken silver from the Temple, which caused the devout Jewish people to riot in the city.

Thousands of people had lost their lives in the carnage. Lazarus was one of them. Mary had been helping a church in Rome when she received the news. If she had stayed near Jerusalem, like her brother had begged, she would have died by his side.

Fresh tears wet her cheeks.

Then she broke out in a hysterical laugh until her sides burned. It was several moments before Mary could compose herself. She remembered back to her father's funeral. Martha had privately scorned her for spending too much money on their burial.

Lazarus' young words echoed in her mind from long ago, "We are only going to bury him once, you know."

"Well, my dear brother." Mary laughed again for a few moments. "I guess some of us have the honor of being buried twice." She chuckled at the thought. Then the sadness took over again and she began to weep. "Only this time, Jesus is not here to raise you."

Mary wept and moaned for her brother while she pounded on the stone. "I wish I had listened to you. I wish I had stayed here to be with you."

Then a familiar peace washed over her as she went back to the thought of Jesus. A smile crossed her lips.

"At least you are with him now, dear Lazarus." Mary slid down the stone and sat in the dirt. "All of you are. Except me." She brushed her fingertips against the large rock. "But one day we will all be together again."

As the sun set, Mary gathered herself up off the ground and headed to her house. She looked around the courtyard and realized just how much she would miss the sound of her brother moving about the house.

Then she heard a knock at the front door. Opening it, she saw a handful of women standing there staring at her. All of them were dressed in black and trying to hold smiles of sympathy on their worn faces.

She welcomed them in and showed them to the kitchen as Mary silently thanked God for providing for her in her time of need.

"You always know just what I need." Mary smiled up at the ceiling, knowing that God was listening to her and that He was probably smiling too.

At The Church

"And Jesus went out, and departed from the temple: and his disciples came to him for to shew him the buildings of the temple. And Jesus said unto them, 'See ye not all these things? verily I say unto you, There shall not be left here one stone upon another, that shall not be thrown down.' "
-MATTHEW 24:1-2

A.D. 70, Ephesus

"It was awful," Mary wept in the open doorway. Her ashen face was soaked with tears. Her dress was covered in dust from running most of the way for days from Bethany to Ephesus.

"Come in and sit down." John waved her to a place.

"It's terrible. Just terrible."

"You're safe now," John said, passing her a cup of cool water.

"Just awful." Her hands shook around the cup. She spilled some on her chin as she took a sip and then put it down. "There was so much screaming and fire. John, the fire burned so large."

"From the beginning, tell me what happened."

"A few years ago, when Gessius Florus took the silver from Temple, it started a war. He sent soldiers into the city and killed so many people." Mary's shoulders heaved. "They killed Lazarus."

"I'm sorry. I knew things were getting bad in Jerusalem and that Rome's hatred towards our people was on the rise. I knew it was only a matter of time before something happened." He shook his head. "At least I've been able to set up places for believers to gather in these outer regions. Jesus told us to go. It just took a little encouragement," John chewed on the word. "To get some of us going."

"At least Lazarus died fighting the way he wanted to live." She smiled at the thought of Lazarus and Jesus meeting again. "He didn't get that chance for most of his life."

"I received word here."

"Florus was eventually replaced, but the revolt had already started. A group of zealots charged their fortress at Masada. The whole city of Jerusalem went mad. They started killing Roman troops." Mary took a breath. "Then the Romans came in force. For months, they fought in the city. There was so much death. General Vespasian began calming the outlying regions and had his eyes on Jerusalem."

"Then, Nero died."

"Yes. Vespasian's people wanted him to take

over as Emperor. He sent Titus to deal with the rebellion. By now, no one could get in or out of the city. I stayed in Bethany and prayed."

John nodded in understanding. "I spent much time in prayer as well."

"Then the machines came."

"Machines?"

"These giant structures that threw boulders at the walls. I could hear them all day." A shiver ran through her body. "It didn't take long before they made it through the walls. Smoke rose high from the city. The large, dark clouds hung over it. I saw a large smoke pillar coming from where the Temple stood. With the Romans' rage, it wouldn't surprise me at all if not one stone was-"

"-was left on another," John picked up her words.

She tilted her head.

He met her eyes. "You don't remember?"

Mary searched her memory, but came up empty.

"Jesus told us. 'Not one stone will be left on top of another. Every one of them will fall.' We asked him later what he meant. He explained some of the signs of his coming."

"Yes! I remember now."

"He told us so much that we didn't understand," John said. "He even told us we wouldn't understand until later."

Mary took a few deep breaths. "When I saw the smoke coming from the city, I packed what I could carry and just started running." Her heart finally slowed. "I kept walking from town to town until I got here to Ephesus. I remembered you had settled here and came to find you. I'm so tired."

"Rest," John said. "I will make sure you're safe. I'm sure the last thing the Romans are looking for is an old Jewish woman."

Mary laughed with her lessening fear. "Do you remember when you and Peter and the others came back from Galilee?"

"Yes."

"You told us about what Jesus said to Peter."

He nodded.

"What did he say to you? There were so many rumors."

"I've heard them, but that's not what he said."

"Tell me."

"I followed behind Jesus and Peter. I thought he was going to leave again. I wanted to keep my eyes on him. He was telling Peter how he was going to die."

"He was right."

"He always is. Anyway, he was describing how Peter would die when Peter noticed me following them. He asked Jesus about me."

"Why would he ask about you?"

John shrugged. "He told him not to worry about me. He asked Peter if he chose to keep me alive until he came again, what business was it to Peter. He was trying to get Peter to focus on his own walk. He would have a hard path."

"That makes sense now. Everyone thinks you're not going to die."

"But he said 'if.' He wasn't saying he would keep me alive until he came, but if he did, that wouldn't have an effect on Peter and his walk."

"I see." She looked up to see him studying her.

"I was wondering if you could answer something for me."

"I'll try."

"That night in the garden."

"Yes?"

"You were there, weren't you?"

Mary nodded.

"I thought I saw you in the shadows."

"It was my garden after all."

"Yes, Jesus told us. That night, the one in which he was betrayed. I thought I saw…"

"An angel," Mary finished his thought.

"So, it *was* one."

"Yes. He was very real and very beautiful."

John shook his head. "I would have wagered I was dreaming."

"He was ministering to Jesus. They were whispering to each other."

"I have so much guilt about that night. If we had stayed awake, then maybe. Just maybe."

"It wouldn't have changed anything. It was meant to happen the way it did."

"Hmm." He stroked his white beard.

"You're only human, John. All of you had been up all day preparing for the meal. You spent all night feasting, singing, and listening to Jesus teach. With a full stomach and an overwhelmed mind, any man would have fallen asleep. It was very late."

John nodded quietly to himself for a few moments. "I'm going to tell your story."

Mary tilted her head.

"I know you testified for Luke."

"That was some time ago."

"Precisely. I want to clear up the confusion about you. People don't believe it was you who anointed Jesus."

"Luke was merely trying to protect me. We were under a time of great persecution like we are now. He was afraid that mentioning me by name would put me in great danger. It doesn't matter now."

"It does matter," John insisted. "Jesus prophesied that your story would live on as a testimony for you and what you did."

"I remember."

"You were the only one who understood what Jesus was saying. You knew he was going to die. How did you know?"

"Know?"

"What was going to happen?"

"I just...did. It all began to make sense. Though I had no idea how it was going to end." She thought on all Jesus had taught. "I understood he would let himself be taken and sacrificed. I just had no idea to what extent and that He would be resurrected. It reminds me of Abraham."

"Oh?"

"Yes. Abraham told his servants that he and his son were going up the hill to worship and he and the boy would return. If he was obeying God's call to sacrifice his son, then why did he said the boy would return with him?"

John thought. "He had faith."

"Yes, he had faith that God would keep His word. No matter what happened on that mountain, Isaac would still be the promised one to bring about a great nation. Abraham didn't know the how, just the outcome that God had promised. He believed what God had told him for the beginning and the end. Abraham had absolute faith that God would handle the middle."

"I see."

"That's how I felt. I knew what Jesus was saying, even though I didn't know how he was going to do it. I was trusting God with what would happen on the mountain." She thought about all the teaching she had committed to memory. "Besides, he told us several times."

"But none of us heard him. We were listening, but we didn't want to hear it. Especially me."

"Stop being so hard on yourself. You were young and full of vigor."

"A son of thunder." He grinned.

"Exactly. You still have that same fire." She found the old light in his eyes.

"Unfortunately, we are in the minority in our

world."

"I know. I came to warn you. Word is floating around that they are coming for you. Domitian wants your head."

"He can have it. Jesus has my soul."

"Be serious."

"I am. I'm not going to stop being a witness just because some Roman tells me to." John huffed and then adjusted his old frame. "There are so many gone now. They stoned Jesus' own brother, James."

"I know."

"Phillip was crucified, as was Peter. Andrew was tied to a cross and hung there two days in which he told anyone who passed by about Jesus. James, my brother-" John wiped away the dampness from his face. "So many have sacrificed their lives for the souls of others. I was supposed to be a simple fisherman."

"You are a fisherman, remember?" She smiled.

"A fisher of men." John had a good laugh and then wiped away a tear. "He is always right."

Mary calmed her laughing. "I'm worried about you."

"All in God's will, remember?"

Mary nodded. "I'd like to stay here in Ephesus. If that's alright."

"I think they would welcome you warmly."

She smiled.

"Now," he said, as he picked up a metal stylus and straightened a piece of parchment on the table in front of him. "Let's start at the beginning."

Hours later, confident that she had once again told her story, Mary left John's home in the cool night air. She had testified of God's glory and goodness. She recounted the many blessings of being at Jesus' feet. She held to the peace in her soul that she was exactly where God had placed her.

When she reached the nearby Inn that John told her about, she removed her headscarf and washed. She laid her head down on a straw mat. Her bones ached with age. She inhaled slowly and whispered into the night, "Praise you, Lord." With the familiar warmth filling every part of her being, she closed her eyes.

At The End

"Whom have I in heaven but thee? and there is none upon earth that I desire beside thee."
-PSALM 73:25

In The Meadow

Mary opened her eyes to find herself lying in an open field of wildflowers. Certain she was having some fantastic dream, she laid still and let the sun warm her face.

"Mary," a voice called from somewhere.

She jumped up and looked around for the source of the voice. Spinning in every direction, she searched for his face.

"Mary."

She smiled and turned around.

There he was, standing in all his glory a short distance away from her. His face shined brighter than a hundred suns. Even at that distance, she could tell he was smiling.

Mary ran to him.

In her haste, she fell to her knees, landing at his feet. She didn't care. It was probably where she was going to end up anyway.

"Master," she cried and bowed her forehead to the wonderfully green grass. It was soft on her skin like young lamb's wool.

She raised her head to look into his deep brownish-black eyes. They shone like two Judean Iris flowers in the morning light.

He extended his hands down to her.

She embraced the offer to stand.

As she slid her palms into his open hands, he moved his palms down her forearms to grip her elbows in order to offer more support. Her hands naturally slid down his arms in response and she felt something change in the smoothness of his skin. Looking down, she noticed the raised scars that lay just under the place where his palms and forearms met.

Letting go of his left hand, Mary reached for his right hand. She brushed her fingertips along the scar and stared into the hole left by the spike. She glanced up into his eyes as a single tear fell down her cheek.

He smiled sweetly at her. Reaching up, he carefully brushed the wetness from her face with his free hand.

She held his hand against her face and rubbed it against her cheek. Closing her eyes, she thought about how soft his skin was. It was the softest thing she had felt in her entire life. Curious for a craftsman.

"Greetings, Jesus."

He pulled her in close.

She couldn't be sure, but she was almost positive she could smell Spikenard on his olive skin. The smile deepened on her face as the memory of that day so long ago, when she anointed his body with the precious oil, came flooding over her like a cool wave.

He suddenly held her out to arm's length and looked deep into her eyes. "Welcome home, dear one. Welcome home."

"Home?" Mary asked with a tilt of her head. She gazed around the beautiful field and then back at him. "You mean I'm not dreaming?"

Jesus shook his head. "No, my dear. It was finally time for you to come home," he said and pulled her in close for another embrace. "I promised you one day nothing would separate us," he whispered into her hair. "That day has come."

This time, as Mary held on tight to him, she was sure it was Spikenard she could smell on him.

Want to find out what happens next?

Lea and Timothy desired a simple life together, but they couldn't ignore the call of God.

Lea wanted a modest, married life like her older sisters. When her betrothed, Timothy leaves on another missionary journey with his mentor Paul, Lea doesn't know when he will return to take her as his wife. If he does, will she continue to support him even though it means possibly spending their lives apart?

The Romans aren't making it easy to be a Way follower and neither is her family. With opposition on every side will Lea bend to the pressure or continue to stand on her newfound faith?

Find out if they will risk it all for the gospel in Book 6 of the Faith Finders Series, *Lasting Legacy*.

Also by Jenifer Jennings

Special Collections and Boxed Sets

Biblical Historical stories from the Old Testament to the New, these special boxed editions offer a great way to catch up or to fall in love with Jenifer Jennings' books for the first time.

The Rebekah Series: Books 1-3
Faith Finder Series: Books 1-3
Faith Finders Series: Books 4-6
Servant Siblings Series: Books 1-3
Servant Siblings Series: Books 4-7
Paul's Patrons Series: Books 1-3
Paul's Patrons Series: Books 4-6

* * *

The Rebekah Series:

Follow Rebekah on her faith journey from the fields of her homeland to being part of Abraham's family.

The Stranger
The Journey
The Hope

* * *

Faith Finders Series:

Go deeper into the stories of these familiar faith heroines.

Midwives of Moses
Wilderness Wanderer
Crimson Cord
A Stolen Wife
At His Feet
Lasting Legacy

* * *

Servant Siblings Series:

*They were Jesus' siblings,
but they become His followers.*

James
Joseph
Assia
Jude
Lydia
Simon
Salome

* * *

Thank You!

My Family: Thank you for stepping up in everything, so that I can do what I love to do. I couldn't do any of this without you. Love you!

Jenifer's Jewels (ARC Team): Thank you for such a great response to this story. You guys and gals rock!

Word Weavers Clay County: You gals are awesome! Thank you for helping the incredible journey of this novel.

About the Author

Jenifer Jennings is a passionate storyteller who brings ancient worlds to life through Biblical historical novels. A devoted student of Scripture since coming to faith in Jesus at seventeen, she holds a bachelor's degree in Women's Ministry and a master's in Biblical Languages. Jenifer is an active member of Word Weavers International, serving as an online chapter president, and a member of American Christian Fiction Writers (ACFW). When Jenifer's not writing, she's on a date with her husband or mothering their two children, a wise-cracking mathematician and a feisty artist.

If you'd like to keep up with new releases, receive spiritual encouragement, and get your hands on a FREE book, then join Jenifer's Newsletter at:
jeniferjennings.com/gift